MW01205288

Bar Stories

4/2000

David —
Happy (Future) Birthday
I hope you enjoy my
contribution to your
porn collection
— Courtney

Bar Stories

Edited by Scott Brassart

alyson books
los angeles | new york

© 2000 BY ALYSON PUBLICATIONS. ALL RIGHTS RESERVED.

MANUFACTURED IN THE UNITED STATES OF AMERICA.
COVER DESIGN BY B. ZINDA.

THIS TRADE PAPERBACK ORIGINAL IS PUBLISHED BY
ALYSON PUBLICATIONS,
P.O. BOX 4371, LOS ANGELES, CALIFORNIA 90078-4371.
DISTRIBUTION IN THE UNITED KINGDOM BY
TURNAROUND PUBLISHER SERVICES LTD.,
UNIT 3 OLYMPIA TRADING ESTATE, COBURG ROAD, WOOD GREEN,
LONDON N22 6TZ ENGLAND.

FIRST EDITION: DECEMBER 1999

00 01 02 03 04 **a** 10 9 8 7 6 5 4 3 2 1

ISBN 1-55583-536-8

LIBRARY OF CONGRESS CATALOGING-IN-PUBLICATION DATA
  BAR STORIES / EDITED BY SCOTT BRASSART.
    ISBN 1-55583-536-8
    1. GAYS—BIOGRAPHY. 2. GAY BARS. I. BRASSART, SCOTT.
  HQ76.25.B37 1999
  306.76'62'0922—DC21   99-042062

COVER PHOTOGRAPHY BY THOM LANG/THE STOCK MARKET.

Contents

Do You Believe I Love You? by Kevin Bentley 1

The Smoiff Collection by Blaise Bulot 16

Taking in the Anchor by Christopher Horan 18

My Night Tonight by Bob Condron 27

The New Me by Jim Piazza 35

A Turkey Bar Plucking by Dean Durber 41

No-Fun Club Kid Turns 30 by Mark Macdonald 46

Patron of the Arts by Jack Fritscher 51

Bully in a Bar by Gregg Shapiro 56

Post-Communist Bar Trilogy by Ernest McLeod 72

Who is Hansen Waiting For? by Gene Michael Higney 91

My First Pickup Line by Ethan Brandon 97

Bless You, Bella by Duc DeForge 101

Halloween Drag by Christopher Lucas 108

No Choices (Keine Auswahl) by Owen Levy 116

Midnight in the Garden of Evil by Joe Frank Buckner 122

An Amsterdam Night by David May 133

The Catalyst by Brian Cochran 139

Roosters at the Seashore by Michael A. White 148

Backroom News by Wayne Hoffman 153

Beasts in the Burbs by Mark C. Abbott 157

Adventure at the Phoenix by Blaise Bulot 162

Night Town by Randy Clark..165

Rocky I, II, III, IV, V by Chip Livingston 174

Five Nights by Ian-Andrew McKenzie...............................182

Once on Christmas Eve by J. G. Hayes 191

In Search of Local Wildlife at the Gizmo Lounge by Ron Suresha ..195

One for the Road by M. Christian 207

Contributor Biographies 210

Preface

When I sent out the call for *Bar Stories,* I expected to receive a tidal wave of submissions—and I did. What I didn't expect was variety. I thought nearly every story would describe a backroom sexual encounter or a pickup leading to a sexual encounter. A few of the submissions were exactly what I expected, and the best of those are included in this anthology.

The remainder, however, surprised me. I received a large number of extremely interesting, well-written, nonsexual stories. And so, much to my delight, the direction of the collection changed from "erotic" to "literary."

If you bought this book hoping for something sexy, don't despair. *Bar Stories* does contain, as mentioned above, several very sexy stories. But for the most part, it is a panoramic view of that worldwide bastion of gay socialization—gay bars—told from both a big city and a rural perspective, with stories from all over North America, Europe, and even Japan. As such, it is my hope that this volume will succeed not only as queer entertainment but also as a literary sociological examination.

Scott Brassart
Los Angeles, 1999

Do You Believe I Love You?
by Kevin Bentley

When I saw him on the street that day, a hollow-eyed, shuffling Nosferatu, I knew he'd be turning up in the trickle of
obits in the *Bay Area Reporter* before you could say "Coming
Home Hospice." I hadn't seen Sam in 15 years; if I'd thought
of him recently, I'd have assumed he was already dead or had
moved back to Tennessee.

We don't die of love, of course, though for a very long
while, a lot of us were popping off regularly from something
tragically associated with it. I came near to dying of love for
Sam, though, or thought I did—twice.

It's said that many gay men in the '70s and early '80s attempted to lead the lives of boy-crazy teenage girls they'd en-
vied during adolescence. This was true of me. I was a 25-year-
old adult male employed as a paperback buyer in a downtown
San Francisco bookstore, but standing behind the register, bel-
lying up to a bar, or jumping about on a blinking dance floor,
I still saw myself as that brainy, well-behaved 16-year-old—the
sedate Hayley twin in *The Parent Trap*—ready to worship slav-
ishly at the altar of the first self-assured, not-so-smart, sexually
aggressive man who chose to pull off my glasses and push me
down onto a dirty mattress.

I logged my tricks and affairettes in a fairly cold-blooded journal, but tellingly cut out and glued on the flyleaf a campy frame from a romance comic of a girl weeping into her pillow beneath the legend: "And sometimes, even when I just dreamed about Bill with another girl, I cried in my sleep."

It was July of '81, and I had just reread the complete novels of Jean Rhys—so it should have come as no surprise that when a slim, hard, ex–sheet-metal worker from Tennessee sidled up to me one Sunday at the End-Up and asked me to dance, my smart mouth and good sense evaporated in the heat of his blue gaze, and I embarked on an ecstatic and painful interval of utter, craven bondage.

My life has been defined by a series of Sundays. Depressing memories of forced marches to Baptist church and Sunday school are never completely banished—along with the hateful boredom of our stale suburban tract house afterward as my parents napped or played Aggravation at the kitchen table. Later there were manic Sundays spent with straight pals, driving around aimlessly, drinking Schlitz, or hiking around the Ice Age rock formations at Hueco Tanks, tripping on windowpane acid we melted beneath our eyelids for a faster, nausea-free high. Then came life in Mecca, and Sundays were either an Elysium of lazy days in bed or at the movies with the latest boyfriend or an existential nightmare of staring at the phone and weeping, trying to pretend that lying on the couch all evening reading an Iris Murdoch novel cover to cover constituted a life.

If you passed through Friday and Saturday nights without meeting someone or if, as was the case with my best friends Gary and Michael, you weren't getting along that well with the lover you had, Sunday afternoons and evenings were the worst. Michael would call me up to go dancing at noon.

"What else were you planning to do—slit your wrists?" he'd ask in his world-weary Florida drawl. This remark, ritually made, bears a certain weight, since five years later Michael did kill himself. This was back in Florida after Gary died; Michael had confided his HIV status to a restaurant coworker and was promptly fired. He borrowed his dad's car and rifle, drove somewhere secluded, and blew his head off. I imagine it was a Sunday.

Michael and Gary got me into the habit of going to the End-Up on Sundays—or *church*—as everyone called it, with a nod to our common Sunday phantoms. We'd meet at Powell and Market and go racing down Sixth Street, stepping around passed-out drunks and pools of urine. Approaching Sixth and Harrison, I felt the bass throb at the same moment I saw the ugly brown-trimmed building with the crooked white plastic letters. That first glimpse always made me think of the Sugar Bowl Nightclub in Fearless Fly cartoons—the walls physically pulsing and swelling with the music as the syncopated patrons streamed in.

When you stepped inside you felt the chill of ice—ice in bins behind the big rectangular bar, crushed ice regularly dumped into the steaming urinals—warring with the wet, insinuating heat of the big raised dance floor, where people with flushed damp faces or sunken-eyed tripping-all-night faces stomped and spun and windmilled their arms. We'd dance, drink 35-cent draft beer from plastic cups, sit outside in the sun drying off, and then dance again till our T-shirts were stained with salt and our hair stuck out however it dried. For those hours I was happy: laughing, confident of my looks and at ease in my body, delivered from the Sunday horrors.

As anyone who drinks and has taken recreational drugs can tell you, when it's fun it's great fun, and when it goes wrong

it's awful. Many of those Sundays ended badly, when I'd drink
too many beers and stalk out after cross words with Gary or
Michael, sleepwalking into the parking meters along Sixth
Street. Or I'd swallow some offered capsule with youthful in-
souciance and later, too high for speech or eye contact, rush
home in terror and ride it out in bed with the blinds down,
ready to swear off everything if I could only have back my
sharp, sober mind. On those convalescent evenings the hyp-
notic ticking of the *60 Minutes* stopwatch on a poorly tuned
black and white TV gave a kind of soul balm.

It was on one of the happy days that I noticed Sam eyeing
me. "Do you know what a beautiful smile you have?" he said,
leaning close in the loud bar. I was aware only of his clear blue
eyes; his shiny, straight white teeth; and the fact that he was
drenched with sweat and smelled good—ferny, fecund, like
clean but damp privates.

Gary, nearby, was less star struck. "You smell dick, you
mean. That guy lives here. He's a lying sack of shit with all that
cornpone sincerity. You'd better look out."

We danced together for several hours. Sitting out back against
the high fence that blocked a freeway ramp, we drank our foam-
ing, tepid beers. People around us shrieked with laughter or restlessly cruised while carrying on bored conversation.

His name was Sam Warren; he was 30 years old; and he'd
only come to San Francisco from Tennessee a few months before, leaving behind an ex-wife and two little boys—but he
wanted to get custody of the kids and bring them out to California, he said. While I was telling him about myself, he
leaned over and deftly licked my wet forehead. Then he kissed
me, and I gave myself over to kissing back, with ridiculously
pounding heart and hollow stomach. When he broke away
and returned to his cigarette with a satisfied smile, the first

thing I saw was Gary, glaring at me from across the patio like a gargoyle.

We didn't go home together till the following Sunday, which gave me a week to torture myself with wondering if he'd really show up again and whether my impression of him wasn't utterly misremembered. As with all divine visitations, I'd been blinded, and I couldn't really recall his face—only how I'd felt.

He did come, and in the early evening I brought him to my studio above the Stockton Steps. When we'd sat a few minutes on the old green vinyl couch and he'd smoked a cigarette, he leaned back and smiled crookedly at me, stretching his legs out. Only a little light filtered through the ivy framing the one big window. His delicate features, golden mustache, and longish light-brown hair reminded me of the *Mud Slide Slim*–era James Taylor.

"Take your clothes off," he said quietly. Outside, the fog had begun to roll in; the foghorns were doing their muffled bellowing. And as I pulled off my purple high-tops and T-shirt and jeans, I started to tremble. We kissed, then he pushed me off and stood up. "Take it out," he said, staring hard at me. I fumbled his belt buckle and stiff new button-flies open.

Maybe Gary was right, and I had been smelling dick. It was very erect. It stuck straight out and up, jerking when I touched it, and gave off a slightly sweet, mushroomy, mulchy odor attributable, I thought, to the bit of pale, retracted hood. It wasn't especially large, but as befitted the most beautiful man I'd ever seen, he had what seemed to me a perfect penis: marble-white, smooth and hard, not bumpy and gristly, a just-discernible blue vein pulsing beneath the skin right up to the corona, and a thick, flushed head—all pointing up and jabbing at the air like a gesturing dictator.

The exhaustive range of that first night's lovemaking was

quickly honed to the essential. On those few occasions when I was allowed to penetrate Sam, he lay motionless on his stomach, fists clenched, and endured with a sort of grim air of accomplishment. His top abilities were subtler and more erotic than the overt professionalism of the left-hankied muscle queens (who danced with stiff chopping and squatting motions, as if moving phantom weights). Sam swung his hips and wrists unselfconsciously on the dance floor, and he fucked like it was as necessary as breathing, raining kisses and endearments onto me with an almost feminine hysteria. While Sam fucked me or as we drifted off to sleep, folded into each other afterward, he uttered the most heartrending expressions of need and tenderness I'd ever heard. I hadn't had such romantic sex with a man before, and it was strong stuff.

A twist that quickly brought me to a condition of combined resentment and helpless, slobbering attraction, like the hypnotist's subject in a cartoon, was Sam's out-of-bed stance that sex was the thing I needed, like a sick boy needs his medicine, to be doled out patiently and deliberately. It irked me that someone clearly in need of lots of sex, who had to have it and went out compulsively looking for more of it when he wasn't with me, kept up the charade that I was insatiably trying to "get a piece" off him.

Looking at Sam's tall, wiry frame; the '60s schoolboy side part and the light-brown bangs hanging across his eyes; the untucked, tapered plaid Sears shirts, sleeves rolled up to the elbow; the badness and swagger, I was overcome with a devotion that went straight back to my adolescence. My older brother spent two years teaching me to want sex, then turned 15, got a motorcycle, and shunned me, a faggot-to-be. Sam embodied my brother and every cool eighth-grade hood who'd ever cupped his crotch and sneered at me. He was no good. Everyone said so. He said so himself, part of his rap when he got high. "You're gettin' too serious about me, honey. I love you, but I'm afraid you're gonna get hurt. You'll hate me one day."

Sam had a sidekick and caretaker, Harlan, who had preceded him in an earlier scouting party of gay men from Nashville and who had also found him his job as a maintenance man at a huge mall outside the city. (I never let myself even think the word *janitor*. Besides, he made more than I did selling books, and I wasn't averse to having a boyfriend who stood around at work in a gray uniform with "Sam" stitched in red cursive writing over the same pocket that held his pack of Kool menthols—who popped a tall Bud as he came through the door and fretted about being late with his child support.) Harlan was plump and not always quite clean, speaking confidentially in my ear with sour beer breath while his big, slightly jaundiced eyes ticked over the passing men. He had the evil chuckle of a much fatter man and an almost unintelligible drawl. He was a sort of disco Burl Ives. Gary, who made lurid faces behind his back at the End-Up, dubbed him the Stewed Chicken. Harlan wheezed about Sam's bad exploits over the kitchen table while we both pretended we didn't know Sam was shooting up in his bedroom or at my side in a dance bar while I nervously watched to see who Sam was dancing with.

Harlan filled me in on Sam's departure from Tennessee. He'd been shooting up speed and MDA so often he got fired from his job with an exterminator, amid threats of prosecution for stealing prescription drugs from clients' medicine cabinets. He attempted suicide with some of his booty but was saved at the last moment by Harlan, who nursed him back to functional health and brought him to San Francisco after Sam swore he'd never shoot up again.

We fell into seeing each other regularly, usually spending Thursday through Sunday nights together, always Sunday afternoons at the End-Up. Though Sam had vigorously pursued me, I soon found that for all his talk of love, he was not to be pressed for the slightest commitment. He considered us both entirely free to have sex with others whenever we liked. "Do you want to know how many guys I've been with since I met you?" he asked after the first month, to my horror. "I'm not gonna lie to you." Sam didn't approve of jealousy. "I better not ever catch you acting jealous, or that'll be all she wrote!" I couldn't make out how he could love me as much as he crooned in my ear each night, how he could phone me every day to tell me so and call me his little pumpkin nose and then bring someone else home—but though I was besotted and obsessed, I knew that I held a minority viewpoint in 1981 San Francisco, and I tried to believe I was being childish and unreasonable.

Most of the time I went to Sam's place to spend the night. The Victorian flat he shared—with its tilting, creaking floorboards beneath the cheap carpet—had been gutted in a fire, and the quick makeover hadn't banished the acrid smell of charred wood and mildew that seeped from behind the new paint. The odor, the then-scary Hayes Valley side street, and the manic lives of Harlan and the other occupants lent an air of impending disaster, orchestrated with sirens and car alarms.

The fainting room that served as Sam's bedroom had just enough space for a double bed and the giant birdcage that held his white cockatiel. (I suspected that in his first weeks in the city, he'd been one of those *Swiss Family Robinson* clones you used to see strutting around with unsanitary-looking parrots on their shoulders.) Sam was no more responsible a pet owner than he was a parent; I never saw him take the bird out or feed it, though there was food—or the cracked husks of it—spread over every inch of the room. I'd wake in the icy night to the screech and flap of the bird, Sam flipping on the overhead light in time for us to see mice diving from the bottom of the cage and running in all directions. He would smoke a cigarette then, my head on his hip, stroking my hair and mumbling his litany of endearments—"Honey, you scare me, you know that? My little petunia nose"—while bottles smashed and screams rose from the alley beyond the dark window dripping with condensation.

I stared at that same high, rattling window the day I let him shoot me up. It was a cool, foggy Saturday morning. Sam had been in vibrating good spirits the night before; he'd scored a bunch of crystal at work and had already hit up twice in one of his subterranean hiding places at the mall before he got on BART to head home. I woke to find him propped on his elbow and smoking ruminatively, staring at me.

"Do you know how much I love you?" he said. "You're going to shoot up with me—OK? I'll only give you a little." He got up, locked the door, and dug the green metal toolbox out from under the dirty clothes piled in the closet. I'd watched him do it often enough. He melted the crystal in a spoon with a little water, tied off my arm, and filled a clean syringe, holding it up to the light and tapping it reverently. I felt overwhelming love—and terror. I felt I was letting him take my life, and I wanted to let him do it. He pushed his smoky tongue in my mouth for a moment, then sat back and stuck me.

I was looking away from the needle, staring at his handsome, intent face. Then sudden heat illuminated me like an atomic flash, and with supreme effort I turned my head to see the window where so much light was coming from. A high-frequency buzz started up in my ears and shot down my spine, and the wall and window blew in and snapped in my face like wash on a line, and I thought, *This must be what dying is like.* For a while

I wasn't even aware of Sam, who quickly injected himself and lay beside me on the bed. The next thing I noticed was a sharp, funky odor: We were both shivering and bathed in a sweat so profound, even the soles of my feet were slick.

Being with Sam—being in love with him, taking drugs with him—comprised a whole other existence from the life I lived away from him. Around Sam I was happy but apprehensive; I was the Boyfriend, but for how long? Ivy Street, the omnipresent disco mixes, the disco-bunny culture of his few friends and roommates—all were in stark contrast to my Stockton Street studio, bookstore friends, and the Elvis Costello and Go-Go's I listened to. I *was* Heathcliff, all right, but my Heathcliff stood in a copse of bar stools, and instead of the wind whistling over the moors, there was only the thump and falsetto of "Disco Man."

Most of the story was played out on his turf: the slanting-floored Ivy flat, the End-Up, another seedy morning-after bar called the Balcony. He wouldn't come over for dinner, wouldn't meet my friends. If I said yes to some outing with my own friends on a weekend night, I'd spend the evening imagining Sam out getting high and tricking with someone. Away from him, I'd taken to bursting into inappropriate tears, like the tiresome, sobbing girl being ministered to in the back bedroom of every junior high party, distraught because her steady had taken back his ID bracelet and was slow-dancing to "Hey, Jude" with someone else. If I was reckless enough to ask about his evening the next day, Sam would bluntly confess. He'd warned me, hadn't he? "I'll just hurt you, honey!"

Harlan half-heartedly provided cover on those awkward occasions when I called and Sam was actually with someone else. After this happened a few times, I began to find it difficult to get high around Sam. I'd never kept up with him anyway, and now, whether it was smoking a joint at his place or swallowing a cap-sule of MDA outside the End-Up, my jealous worries were dif-ficult to handle. Even after a few beers, I had to be careful. We'd start out affectionate and smiling but end mournfully. He'd dis-appear for too long, and I'd find him in a corner with some guy, slipping a phone number into his pocket. "Don't look at me like that," he'd say. "I told you what I was like."

Sometimes he'd call unexpectedly and ask me to rush over. The passionate love talk still spilled from him during sex, but now it sounded almost belligerent, as if he were daring me to call him a liar. Now when he shot up in front of me, he'd roll his dilated eyes balefully, like a vampire caught slipping back into his coffin. "You're lookin' at me like I was a bug under a microscope," he'd sigh.

I couldn't have been more than 6 years old when my pret-ty teenage Aunt Janet broke up with her boyfriend Chris. She slashed her hand breaking the glass in his framed senior picture, cut up the bloodied photo with a pair of scissors, and flushed it down the toilet. Later, I traced with my finger where her best friend Patty had written in cursive swirls over a yearbook photo of Janet gazing sadly off Scenic Drive: "Don't jump, Janet. Chris will come back." I swooned and knew I'd be scorched by love one day.

Lying in bed, Sam told me in awed tones about his younger sister Lisa, whose husband cracked up when she left him. He showed up one day with a gun and made Lisa strip while he rattled off her infidelities, their two toddlers crying and cling-ing to her legs. Then he put the gun in his mouth and pulled the trigger.

There was drama—public tears! Storming out of bars! We fought one Saturday, and I ran out of his place, slamming the door and heading straight for Polk Street, where I got drunk,

BAD NEWS stamped across my forehead, in hopes of trumping Sam's next infidelity. Passed out later, I didn't answer the phone when it rang, and he charged over and shouldered open my studio door. "I thought you might've tried something crazy," he said, a little let down I thought, and bent me over the foot of the bed while I was still sniffling and wiping my nose on my sleeve. This was both the hottest sex we'd ever had and the precise moment when I knew, behind my delusion, that Sam's strange amalgam of desire and contempt for me had reached its zenith. It was the "Every time I kissed you, I had to wipe my mouth!" moment, as friends and I used to say to each other, mimicking Bette in *Of Human Bondage*.

It wasn't all Mr. Hyde. He used to phone his kids on Saturday mornings, speculating sadly after he hung up as to when he might be able to bring them out. I tried to imagine living somewhere with Sam and helping to parent two shell-shocked little boys, but it was a stretch. He could lie on the couch with an arm around my neck, smoking and watching sitcom reruns with a look of rapt concentration, for hours. But these times—when the omnipresent disco wasn't beating from speakers in every room, when somebody wasn't spreading coke or crystal on a Thelma Houston album cover at the kitchen table, when Sam wasn't bug-eyed and telling me I'd hate him one day—were rare.

We met in July; by October things were grim. He spent a paycheck on MDA, and I didn't see him for a week. I begged him to come over. When he arrived, he sat down on the couch, pulled up his pants leg, and brought out the needle he'd tucked into his sock. "Do you really need to do that?" I asked. He looked at me with infinite fatigue and patience.

"I love you—do you know that? Do you realize how much I love you? Don't you know what you're doin' to me?"

Later, when we took off our clothes and got into bed, I

flinched at the dark hematoma blooming on his arm. He was sweating profusely, too exhausted to get hard. After jerking me off mechanically, he passed out. I lay awake trying to cradle him in our accustomed spoon fashion, but he shuddered and kicked, punching at me in his sleep.

Halloween night: As I rode the crowded bus to Hayes and Laguna, I felt a clear sense of doom about Sam. We'd broken up and gotten back together several times in the last month, one of us panicking each time and calling when the other toughed it out. We'd agreed to spend Halloween together; my old friend David and his boyfriend Dean were driving up from Monterey. They liked Sam because he liked to go dancing and could always get MDA, and they ganged up on me for being jealous. "He loves you, anyone can see that. Stop being so possessive!"

When I walked into the flat, the disco was thumping, and the place was full of the roommates' boyfriends and friends passing joints and drinking beers. I could tell Sam had shot up; he was jittery and joking, smiling at me sheepishly now and then with a quick little nod or wink. Harlan looked at me sympathetically. "You can do a lot better than him, you know," he breathed in my ear. It occurred to me that he knew Sam was already seeing someone else.

David and Dean arrived, and we swallowed capsules of MDA—this was Halloween, after all—and headed for the End-Up. It was odd being there at night; I'd only seen its false-twilit Sunday afternoons. We danced in the jam-packed throng. Sam disappeared for long periods, and I was too high and occupied with David and Dean to bother looking for him. At 2 we moved on to an after-hours club, where for a long while I stood gripped between Sam's knees as he sat on a ledge with his arms around my chest, turning my head to be kissed now and then. I had what I most wanted.

We got back to the flat and crashed at dawn. I woke only a couple of hours later to see Sam injecting himself in the chill morning air, the green toolbox open on the floor. He and Harlan were headed back to the End-Up for the 8 A.M. "leftovers" contest. In the early light the sight of blood rising into the syringe made my balls retract. He cupped my face in his shaking hands. "You know I love you more than anything? You know that, right?"

Around 11, David woke me, and he and Dean and I went back to my place to shower and eat breakfast. If we were up to it, we said, we'd catch up with Sam and Harlan in the afternoon. Driving to the bar several hours later, Dean remembered he'd left his coat at Sam's, and we detoured by Ivy to pick it up. Nobody answered the buzzer, but the door was open, and I bounded up the stairs. The first thing I saw was a dazed-looking blond guy sitting at the kitchen table in his underwear. "Um, hi…?" he said.

"Who's that, Ricky?" Sam called from the bedroom. I pulled Dean's coat off a chair and plunged back down the stairs.

"Take me home," I said. While David and Dean bickered— "But I don't see why we can't go back to the End-Up!"—I hugged my knees in the back seat, trying to remember Natalie's voice-over lines from Wordsworth as she drove away from white-trash Warren Beatty's farmhouse in *Splendor in the Grass*, a parable of bad love absorbed so early, I'd thought it was *splinter*. Bottom had turned back into a man, and I wept bitterly at my release.

Time passed. I went to work and shelved paperbacks. At night I stayed in and read or went out to Polk and Castro bars with Gary and Michael, who were glad to have me back. Sooner or later I'd come home alone and throw myself on the couch and cry till my nose ran and my head ached. I started *After Leaving Mr. Mackenzie* again.

Sam had needed a witness, and it wasn't easy to tear my eyes away from the broken glass and crumpled bodies. A film loop of the flat on Ivy and Sam's room with the squawking bird flickered constantly in the back of my mind. I could see the stoned blond lying on the bed while Sam, grim and pale, heated crystal in a spoon and shot up. I could see Sam framing that blond's face with both hands, like he'd held mine, as he came on to the speed or MDA, nearly passing out, the words tumbling from the drowning man's lips: "Do you believe I love you? Do you believe me?"

After about a month he phoned me at work. "Well, hey there! It's Sam! How're you doin', honey?" He sounded sweet, anxious to talk to me. My stomach dropped; I put the phone back in the receiver and sat on a box of books, Olivia de Havilland heading up the stairs while Montgomery Clift pounded on the bolted door.

He didn't call again. I avoided the End-Up and the Balcony after that, so I didn't run in to him. I saw Harlan once in a bar several years later. "He ain't doing so good," he said, without my asking.

When I saw him moving in slow motion down the opposite side of Castro Street, my stomach didn't turn over and my legs didn't give the way they once did. The street between us yawned like the Rio Grande gorge. Wheeling in that gaping space were two lovers, both dead of AIDS, and the very different requited love and bone grief that had meant. A stream snaked along the bottom of the canyon; that was 15 years of going on living instead of dying for love or grief. And stretched swaying across, held by a few ancient, frayed ropes, one of those jungle bridges from *The Lost World,* full of dangerous gaps and likely to snap at any step: the chance of loving again with the tender, stupid heart of a girl.

The Smoiff Collection
by Blaise Bulot

In the Delgado Museum in City Park, there is a collection of Fabergé easter eggs from the Russia of the czars. In the old Mint at the foot of Esplanade, there are collections of jazz and Mardi Gras memorabilia. Then there is the Historic New Orleans Collection on Royal Street. And further down Royal Street—much further—is the Smoiff Collection.

The Smoiff Collection is housed in the Golden Lantern. The door is always open, but the joint is so murky, the light so dim that a casual visitor could very well miss the collection hanging in the gloom at the far end of the bar. It is a collection of underwear. Men's underwear.

The collector—always referred to in *Ambush* and *Impact* as "the Golden Lantern's own legend"—is Smoiff, the bartender. For Smoiff the true pleasure of a collection is in the collecting. The Smoiff Collection was accumulated—and hopefully is still growing—not by waving a numbered wand or by a cryptic tweak of the nose or scratch of the ear in the London or New York galleries of Sotheby's or Christie's but by more interesting techniques right in the bar.

So how does Smoiff manage this feat of unlikely prestidigitation? Not by brute force, persuasion, or even a miracle. Simply put, when an innocent cutie strays into the bar, Smoiff gets him drunk and takes his underwear.

You see, underneath the bar is a special bottle from which Smoiff pours "stingers" into tiny shot glasses for his, shall we say, donor. Smoiff has never revealed the formula of this potent stuff, but by comparison a hurricane is mere Kool-Aid.

The tipsy boy—as even sober boys will do—inevitably starts to play the machines. Soon he runs out of change, and not long after, he runs out of bills to be changed. Smoiff, so very arch, eventually renews the kid's money—in exchange for his T-shirt. Next, the boy's shoes and socks are transformed into quarters, which also disappear into the machines.

Then it's the pants. The young man, drunk as he is, hesitates. Another stinger. Off slide the Levis.

Needless to say, by now all eyes are fixed on the young gambler. The other patrons begin to chant, "Play naked. Play naked. Play naked!"

It doesn't take long for the machines to gobble up the boy's last quarter. He looks at himself. All that's left are his Jockey shorts. He turns pink. Smoiff comes out from behind the bar. In his hand is—no, not another stinger—the boy's Levis.

"Ah'll trade ya'll yo' jeans fo' yo' briefs."

A Faustian deal. The boy stands dumbfounded.

"Ah'll give ya'll yo' pants back if ya'll give me yo' briefs."

The briefs slide down. An old queen exclaims, "Lawdy! She's exposin' her Temple of Venus."

Smoiff is slow handing over the jeans. But he has what he wanted and can afford to be magnanimous, so he gives the nude boy back not only his pants but also his shirt, shoes, and socks.

And the briefs, to the appreciative applause of the regulars, are added to the Smoiff Collection.

Taking in the Anchor
by Christopher Horan

During my early 20s—the final years of my life in the closet—I held firmly to one resolution: that I would never, ever set foot in a gay bar. I was convinced that crossing the threshold of any establishment frequented by gay men constituted the Point of No Return. That simple act—even more so than actually having sex with another man—would render me officially gay, a card-carrying homosexual.

To adhere to my resolution, I had to remind myself often about the disastrous possibilities. For one thing, such places were certainly unsafe. After all, if you put that many deviants in one room, dim the lights, and start pouring drinks, you're asking for trouble. I imagined all of the men would be dressed as one of the Village People. An inappropriate glance from the Indian to the cop, an off-handed remark from the cowboy to the construction worker, and all hell could break loose. There was no way I was going to get caught in the middle of that.

I also harbored the fear that I simply would not be welcome. Surely everyone in the bar would already know one another, with every man having already staked out his own personal bar stool. These regulars would not take too kindly to a stranger wandering in uninvited. Besides, it wasn't as if I had much to offer. Surely every gay man's taste in men was identical to my own—strong, rugged, older guys. Not familiar with the word *twink*, let alone the notion that some guys actually go for that sort of thing, I resigned myself to the fact that the crowd wouldn't have much use for a skinny, blond, 23-year-old virgin. If the Marlboro men gathered around me, it would be only to point and laugh and show me the door.

The most compelling scenarios that kept me out of the bars, though, involved being "spotted." One of the patrons—a classmate, a second cousin, my mother's hairdresser, my father's mechanic—would recognize me, and it would all be over. My elaborate charade—one I had orchestrated flawlessly for 23 years—would suddenly begin to unravel, and all because I couldn't resist the burning urge to know what was behind the door marked Him-a-Layin.

Of course, I never stopped to assess the logic in this reasoning. It didn't occur to me that in order to expose me, the spotter would have to account for his own whereabouts in the process. Nor had I concocted a viable reason why the informant would feel compelled to pick up a pay phone at the very sight of me and promptly break the news to my family and friends. None of that mattered. All I knew was that these were chances I was not prepared to take.

Like most resolutions, however, mine was destined to fail. As the inevitable loneliness and curiosity of life in the closet became too unbearable, my willpower began to fade. I finally conceded that perhaps I could go into a gay bar—but only if I took some precautions that would reduce the risks. For starters, I could do a little research. I'd flipped guiltily through enough gay travel guides to know that even the most naive traveler could steer clear of some of the more seedy locales. (I had even learned that AYOR meant At Your Own Risk.) I also knew

that I would have to pick a place far, far from home—where
my anonymity would remain intact. Finally, in the summer of
1994, my opportunity arose.

When one of my graduate professors told me about a two-
week summer writing program in rural Holland, I was instantly intrigued, although the chance to hone my technique in
character development or plot structure had little to do with it.
After all, one didn't have to be a seasoned gay traveler to know
what riches the city of Amsterdam had to offer. What better
place to lift my embargo than in this heathen's paradise halfway
around the world? I enrolled in the program and booked a
flight from Boston that would arrive in Amsterdam several days
before the workshop began. The long flight gave me ample
time to study the pages of my new *Gay Guide to Amsterdam*. I
read the descriptions of each bar a dozen times, determined to
make the perfect selection. By the time I checked into the
youth hostel—the guidebook now buried at the bottom of my
backpack, should any of my bunkmates go searching for toothpaste—I had made my choice: the Anchor. The description—
"a laid-back neighborhood spot where locals and tourists mix
with ease"—sounded inviting and disarming.

The other five occupants of my six-bed hostel room were
large, rowdy Eastern European–looking guys. I could not understand a single word of their conversation, but in my para-
noid state I was convinced that every remark and every laugh
was at my expense. "Look at him!" they must have been
shouting. "The American combing his hair! He's going to a
gay bar!"

I dressed quickly and tried to escape unnoticed.

I had studied the map so closely that I knew the route from
the hostel to the Anchor by heart. It should have been a short
walk, but I took several laps around the block, each time try-

ing to catch a glimpse inside the Anchor's frosted windows. I watched several patrons going in and out. They seemed like normal folks, but what did I know? Maybe they had stuffed their leather chaps and riding crops into their backpacks before leaving the bar. After about 20 minutes of surveillance, I decided it was now or never. Besides, I was ready for a drink.

The interior of the Anchor was not what I had expected: not a cowboy hat or Indian headdress in sight, no live sex acts in dark, smoky corners. In fact, it looked like the sort of bar I frequented in Boston. The customers were a mix of men and women, some alone, others in pairs or groups. The room was long and narrow, with small tables lining the walls. In the center of the room stood a long rectangular bar made of dark wood, with a brass glass rack hanging above its perimeter. Two handsome young bartenders pulled wine glasses from the rack and chatted with the customers while pouring pints of ale.

I tried to conceal my quivering knees as I sat on a stool at the opposite side of the bar, facing the door. When the taller of the two bartenders asked me what I wanted to drink, my voice cracked as I said, "Beer, please." He laughed a little—a reaction I had become used to because I looked far younger than 23. Still, this was Europe, for God's sake! 12-year-olds can drink in Europe, right? Apparently not.

"May I see your ID please?" he asked.

That was it. I was done for. He'd take one look at my passport, then jot my name, address, and social security number into a logbook behind the bar. I'd be on permanent record as having patronized an establishment of ill repute. Under some obscure Dutch law, my parents would receive an official letter in the mail: "Dear Mr. and Mrs. Horan—We are obligated under the Homosexual Notification Act of 1856 to inform you that your son Christopher..." But what choice did I have? If I couldn't produce an ID, the seemingly friendly crowd could erupt into full-scale mockery. I imagined them bursting into an elaborate song-and-dance number reserved for underage Americans who tried to buy booze.

So I did it. I gave the bartender my passport. He glanced at it, smiled, and handed it back.

"Boston," he said. "Nice place." Then he poured me a beer. My initial state of panic began to lift. Except for the two guys making out by the jukebox, this place wasn't so different after all. Two old men traded jokes at a table by the window, while a woman with big red hair entertained a group of young men on the other side of the bar. Every now and then the tall bartender would come by and say to me, ."And how's my friend from Boston?" or "Another pint for the Yank?" I was beginning to feel like a regular.

Best of all—could I be imagining this?—the handsome young bar back seemed to be smiling at me. At me! When he walked by with a tray of glasses, I noticed his name tag: MAARTEN. He caught me looking and winked. I smiled and turned away.

A while later the door opened, and in walked one of the largest men I had ever seen. He was at least 6 foot 5 and looked as if he could bench-press a steer. He made my Slavic bunk-mates look like the Von Trapp children. He stepped into the room, raised both arms in the air, and let out what can only be described as a howl. His face reddened as he wailed. Whatever he was screaming in Dutch left the entire room paralyzed. I looked to my tall bartender for an explanation, but he was pale with fear, his arms extended, apparently trying to calm the raving madman, who was now approaching the bartender and gesturing wildly as he ranted.

A young bald man sitting by the door put on his coat and

headed for the exit, but the big guy wouldn't have it. He lunged at the would-be escapee and shoved him against the wall, then pulled the door shut and yelled something that even I knew meant no one was leaving. But the young bald man was persistent—or maybe just stupid—and made another run for the door. Now the hornet was beyond angry. He lifted the bald man by his jacket and tossed him onto the bar like a sack of peanuts. Then he picked up a bar stool and smashed it against the glass rack overhead. Shards rained down on the man, cutting his face and hands. The bartender rushed to help him, which infuriated the giant even more. He swung the bar stool again and again, along the length of the glass rack. Glass flew in every direction. Several customers sobbed in fear. Most had converged on my side of the bar, as far from the lunatic as they could get. Not knowing a word of Dutch, I felt at a terrible disadvantage. Who was this guy? Was this a habit of his—wreaking havoc on gay bars? Was he a serial basher who made it his personal crusade to rid Amsterdam of queers? The red-headed woman, whom I had heard speaking English earlier, cowered next to me. "What's going on?" I asked. She told me that the big guy had found out about the bartender's affair with his lover and had come to settle the score.

I expected Alan Funt to emerge from the supply closet and announce that I was on *Candid Camera*. Was I actually removing shards of glass from my hair and praying for my life because of an all-male love triangle gone awry?

In a moment of heroic or perhaps desperate optimism, I wondered whether I could do something to end this mess. Maybe that's why I had been fated to come here—to talk some sense into the enormous lunatic and save innocent lives. In fact, maybe that's why God had made me gay in the first place. I'd been looking for a noble reason for years, and maybe this perilous situation was it.

But before I could begin the peace talks, the madman climbed over the bar and began to pummel the bartender. I decided my theory was flawed. If God had intended me to stop this bloodshed, he would have blessed me not with the power of reason but with a knack for the martial arts or a membership in the NRA. Clearly, someone else would have to save the day.

The other bartender jumped on the attacker, but it was no use. The big guy punched him square in the nose and tossed him beside the bleeding bald man. The rest of us watched helplessly as the beating continued. I was terrified—not only for the bartender but, selfishly, for myself too. What if this violent hissy fit turned into an all-out massacre? Even those of us who had not slept with the maniac's boyfriend could be slaughtered at any time.

My mind raced with the consequences. Again I thought of my parents, who would learn not only that their only son was killed but killed in a gay bar. My classmates would read about my sordid demise in the newspaper. Many people would say that I got what I deserved. And maybe they were right.

So then and there I reaffirmed my vow. If by some miracle I made it out of there alive, I would never again set foot in a gay bar. If it meant never having to be this terrified again, I'd settle for a loveless marriage with a pack of kids and a repressed libido, thank you very much.

Soon the big guy reappeared holding the bartender's keys. He walked to the door and locked it with a sinister laugh. *This is it,* I thought. *Let the slaughter begin.*

Then, amidst all the commotion, a moment of tenderness. Maarten, the bar back with the warm smile, stood beside me. He put one hand on the back of my neck, and with the other he rubbed my chest. "Don't be frightened," he said. "We're going to be OK."

And even though I could feel Maarten shaking too, I believed him. Something in the touch of his hands on my body assured me this was not an end but a beginning. Suddenly the fact that I was at the mercy of an insanely jealous psychopath didn't matter quite as much. I was still afraid, of course, but I also felt incredibly alive—more alive than I'd felt in a very long time.

The madman turned his back for an instant, and one of the old men dropped to the floor. I thought he had suffered a heart attack. But then he looked up at me and the other hostages and put a finger to his lips. He tapped Maarten on the leg and pantomimed a key turning in a lock. Maarten handed him his key ring, and the old man crawled toward the back of the room. He made his way to the far wall and pressed his hands against a wooden panel between two tables. A secret half door opened, and the old man scurried outside, unnoticed by our captor.

Maarten gave me a nudge. "Follow me," he whispered.

I looked at the bald kid and the two bartenders, all writhing in pain, and shook my head. Just because the old guy made it didn't mean the rest of us would be so lucky. "I can't," I said.

"Yes, you can."

Maarten waited for his chance, then dropped to the floor. I did the same. The escape hatch could not have been more than 20 feet away, but it may as well have been across the Mojave Desert. I kept expecting to feel the leg of a bar stool or an oversized Dutchman crushing my back. But I didn't. Maarten and I reached the door and darted outside to safety.

The old man had already flagged down a police officer and handed him Maarten's keys to the bar. Three police officers burst into the Anchor and emerged minutes later with the big guy in handcuffs. By now a large crowd had gathered outside. The spectators gasped as the three blood-covered victims were taken away in an ambulance. I overheard the old man tell a reporter that the secret door was a throwback to the days when police raided gay bars.

I tried to find Maarten to thank him for his kindness but lost him in the crowd. I even went back to the Anchor the next day, but the front door was boarded up with a sign that read, CLOSED FOR RENOVATION.

Two summers later I walked along a moonlit beach in Mykonos, arm-in-arm with a handsome Dutchman I'd met earlier in the day. I told him about my trip to Amsterdam and that unforgettable night at the Anchor.

"You were there that night?" he asked. Apparently the incident had become legendary in Amsterdam's gay circles.

"I was there," I said, putting one hand on the back of his neck and rubbing his chest with the other.

My Night Tonight
by Bob Condron

A joke from my school days in the north of England. Chemistry class with dreary Mr. Osborne. Anything to relieve the boredom. Jimmy Hanson leaned over my shoulder:

"What do you call two Scottish queers?"

"I don't know."

"Ben Doon and Phil McCavity."

I thought it was hilarious. Jimmy thought so too. Mr. Osborne didn't.

Who would have imagined that a lifetime later I'd be living and working in Scotland, 30 years of age, and coming around to the idea of coming out.

The Waterloo looked like a typical working-class pub. You'll find the like throughout Britain: polished oak and stained-glass windows, mirrors behind the bar, a couple of slot machines, and a video screen displaying a selection of the current pop hits and the odd camp classic. *Discreet* is not the word. Were it not for the gay 'zines tucked away by the window, one could have mistaken it for a straight bar.

I plonked myself onto a bar stool, ordered a beer, and spent the next 30 minutes staring into it. Not daring to look left or

right. Occasionally consulting my train timetable while surreptitiously checking out the clientele. Drinking in the atmosphere. Allowing myself another half an hour. Another beer.
The old Abba song spinning in my head: "Waterloo. Finally
facing my Waterloo..."

I'd gotten the name and location of the bar from the Gay
Switchboard several weeks earlier and filed it away for future
reference, determined to use it. But when?

At the time I was living in a village outside Glasgow, making my sense of isolation all the more acute. But all things work
for good, and in that quiet space I'd sorted through my life. I
knew I had to begin again—and this time in the city.

I traveled to Glasgow in search of an apartment, but sadly, it
was not my day.

The first apartment was a possible flat share. I was hopeful.
I'd spoken with the other tenant over the phone, once again
referred by Gay Switchboard. The apartment complex was in
a converted mill, a Victorian sandstone building beside a canal.
It was all very impressive: well-decorated, elevators to all
floors, plush carpets. Like a lamb to the slaughter, I arrived at
the appointed hour and rang the door bell. First came the dramatic pause, and then, much to my horror, the door creaked
open to reveal a spectral vision swathed in shadow, backlit, and
with a voice that said: "It's one thing to tell people you're gay.
Quite another to say you're a transvestite."

Out of the gloom lurched a stick insect in a blond wig and
long, dangley earrings.

Clive Barker eat your grisly heart out.

The second apartment was a dump in the red-light district.
Enough said.

I was hot. I was bothered. I was disappointed. To be blunt,

I was well and truly fucked off. That was the catalyst. I decided I deserved to treat myself. I'd finally go and do it. I'd summon my courage and stride bravely into the Waterloo. The day couldn't get any worse, could it?

I was roused from inertia by a young bloke who now stood next to me. Stood with difficulty—drunk as a skunk. Ben (for that's what I'll call him) slurred compliments at me, asked if I'd made many friends since I arrived.

"Yes, lots," I lied.

He tried another tactic. He told me about the bar culture and pointed out the clique of regulars who commandeered one end of the bar. It was the end of the bar that offered a clear view of the entrance and, therefore, newcomers. The group was loud, laughing, self-advertising. And incestuous, he told me.

The conversation dried up as I emptied my beer glass. He made his excuses and left. I returned to the shelter of my train timetable. "Another pint, please."

At 9:30 I looked at my watch again. Two hours had flown by. I'd just have one more pint. Half an hour more.

Have you heard the one about the cowboy?

This handsome stranger—a rough, tough, son of a bitch—rides into town. The sun is scorching. His thirst is chronic. So he ties up his horse and swaggers into the first saloon he comes across. As he enters, all activity stops. All eyes turn to him. Unperturbed, he strides to the counter and is just about to order a beer when he notices the sign above the bar. It reads: WE ONLY SERVE HOMOSEXUALS! So he backs out carefully and heads for the next saloon.

The second saloon has no sign above the bar. *Whew, that's a relief,* he thinks, and he's just about to order when he looks down and sees the sign on the counter: WE ONLY SERVE HOMOSEXUALS! Again, he backs out and heads for the next saloon.

The process is repeated at length, until he finds himself on the edge of town at the very last saloon. By now he's desperate for a drink, stumbling along in the full glare of the noon sun. Inside this saloon it's fresh and cool. It's also completely empty save for a lone bar man. The cowboy stumbles toward him. Looks above. No sign. Looks on the counter. No sign. Looks all around. No sign. Runs his fingers over his parched lips: "Good."

Then he sees the small metal plaque on the floor. It's tiny. But on it something's written. He can't make it out. He pushes back his Stetson and squints. Still can't make it out. Finally, he drops to his hands and knees and bends over, closer, until finally the words come into focus. And the sign reads: BRACE YOURSELF!

I nursed my beer. Waiting. With no idea what I was waiting for. One thing is for sure: I wasn't waiting for the return of Ben. But return he did. This time with boyfriend, Phil, in tow. They seemed to believe they were backing a winner and launched into a joint chat-up routine—a gruesome twosome. Both drunk. Ben, taller. Phil, smaller. Brown hair. Both flirting outrageously. A game born of antagonism; a way for each to get at the other, using me as bait. Phil whispered as Ben ordered yet another round, "I wish I'd met you on a night when my partner wasn't here."

I look that desperate? Dream on.

For the next ten minutes, I lost myself in the video screen and tried to decide if I should risk going to the toilet. Immense trepidation. My head filled with horror stories of tea-room debauchery. I wasn't ready for that. Still, my choices were to piss my pants or go to the toilet. Some choice.

Fortunately, Ben and Phil were distracted, so no excuses were necessary when I climbed off my stool and headed for the "Gents." Focusing on my objective. Determined to make my way there without making any eye contact whatsoever. I failed. *He* smiled at *me*. The great, dark man smiled at me. My first thought was, *Is he looking at me? He's too handsome to be looking at me.* But his gaze was shockingly direct, and there was an unmistakable twinkle in his eyes.

The guy was tall, standing head and shoulders above the crowd. Dressed in faded denim, with cropped hair, and the best beard I'd ever seen: thick but trimmed, chocolate-brown, and growing high on his cheekbones, accentuating a blisteringly white smile.

But this spark of interest was quickly extinguished. Ben and Phil hovered around him. The trio appeared to be friends. Ah, well, *so ist das Leben.*

Thankfully, I found the lavatory empty. I heaved a sigh of relief and my cock out of my pants and let flow against the ceramic wall of the urinal, piss running into the grimy gutter and away. Then the door opened behind me, and Phil came in and stood at the far end of the urinal, not five feet away. I heard his fly unzip. I focused solely on the job at hand.

"Pssst!"

I pretended I hadn't heard him.

"Pssst!"

Reluctantly, I looked. And found myself presented with his open fly.

"Oh, yes," I replied, "Father Christmas."

It felt as absurd then as it sounds now. This bloke was showing me the Santa Claus motif on his underpants—and as this was in the month of May, you'll understand why I failed to be impressed. I left without further comment, returning to the bar.

I'd no sooner resumed my place on the bar stool than Phil returned. He spoke briefly with the great, dark man, then hurried out the door.

He inched along the bar beside *me,* but I was wary, resigned, expecting the worst. Suddenly, he smiled again, opened his mouth, and bowled me over. "Are all Scotsman like those two?" he asked in an obvious Irish accent.

My reply came out as a sigh of relief: "No. Thankfully. Most of them are pretty sound. But obviously there are exceptions?" I motioned after Phil. "Where's he gone in such a hurry?"

"His mate threw a wobbler and stormed out in a huff when he followed you into the little boys room." He smiled again, that glorious smile

And I thought, *You're this handsome, and you're Irish?*

It was as if he read my mind. "All the way from Dublin via Berlin. I'm in Glasgow for a weeklong conference." He held out his hand. "The name's Tom."

My straight, Irish friend Sean told me his chat-up line. He asks, "Do you have a bit of Irish in you? No? Would you like a bit of Irish in you?"

I had always had a thing for Irishmen. The accent? Sean describes the accent as a "pussy magnet." Can't be true for me. A dick magnet, maybe? All I know for sure is, I was completely smitten.

He towered over me and my bar stool. A scientist, a doctor in the process of gaining his professorship. Beauty and brains. A big, bad, bearded *Honig Bär.* A real sweetheart. My luck, it seemed, was about to change.

How long did it take me to fall in love with him? Five, ten, fifteen minutes? Was it when he told me he had a boyfriend in

Berlin? I remember thinking, *What a wonderful guy. He didn't have to tell me that.*

And though it was clear from the play of his eyes that he was interested, he never put the make on me. I didn't know whether to be disappointed or relieved. But then again it gave me the space to relax and feel comfortable. Just two guys chatting in a bar, connecting on some real level. The simple pleasure of getting to know each other through talking and talking and talking...

Don't ask me how, but we got around to the subject of our fathers. The conversation took many twists and turns before we hit that tender spot. My eyes filled with tears. He hugged me, and my lips found his. Within the instant the barmaid was slapping the counter in front of us. "Finish up your drinks now, please!" I looked at my watch. It was still half an hour to closing time. Tom and I did a double take and burst out laughing.

Sadly, it really was time for me to go—if I was to catch my train.

Tom said I could stay the night in his room. Sleep over. Only sleep. Mustn't forget the boyfriend back home. I didn't need much persuading. We ordered another round.

Another chat-up line. Tom tells me of the time he went into the George in Dublin. He was standing at the bar when this short guy gives him the none-too-subtle once-over. Lifting his eyes up...and slowly back down, he finally spoke: "You're a big man, aren't ye?" Leaving a dramatic pause, he sucked purposefully on his cigarette. "So," he exhaled with a flourish, "Is everything in proportion?"

Unfortunately for him he never found out.

We must have been drunk. Why else would we have

walked hand in hand through "Stab City" on the way to his hotel? And despite the gawking faces that peered incredulously from passing cars, we arrived some ten minutes later none the worse for wear. A charmed relationship from the start.

Somewhere between the Waterloo and hotel reception, the boyfriend back home was forgotten. By me at least. I couldn't wait to get into his pants. Couldn't wait...

Hours of passionate activity passed quickly, and then came a point where we sat facing each other, legs astride, on his single bed. Curtains thrown back, we were bathed in moonlight. Naked. His face in my hands. His beautiful face in my hands.

And I thought, *It may not have been my day today, but it sure was my night tonight.*

I couldn't see the years ahead. The years we have spent together. In Berlin. Another life. Another lifetime. All I could see was his beautiful, bearded face, the whiteness of his smile.

And I thought, *I will always remember this face, this moment in time.*

And I have. And I do. He reminds me every day. All I have to do is look in his direction.

The New Me
by Jim Piazza

I'm as good in bars as I am at parties. Unless I know everyone in the room and have known them since preschool, I'm Froze-Fruit on a stick—my eyes set in an unblinking stare, my lips cemented to my teeth. My mind tells me this is a radiantly cheerful face. My mind tells me I'm Miss Iowa on laughing gas. My mind, however, is unable to share this good news with anyone else. I have often been mistaken for a life-size artifact, an air-conditioning duct disguised in a checkered flannel shirt.

Given my rare ability to blend in with wall paneling and utility units, I can go to the same bar hundreds of times without wearing out my welcome. No one remembers me from the last time. This is somewhat disconcerting given that my bar of choice, the Candle, is just down the street from my apartment. Most of its patrons are my neighbors. By day I run into them everywhere, and we vigorously nod to each other like magnetic dashboard dolls. But something happens in a bar. Give me loud music, dim lights, a colorful crush of men who appear to be having the time of their lives, and I disappear.

I become a watcher. I rely on the mirror behind the bar. It allows me to view the full spectrum without having to confront it directly. I watch the Candle regulars who drop by for a few

quickies before dinner—or several quickies *instead* of it. I watch
the Miller Lite drunk who's always at his sexiest just before
passing out. His slitted eyes take on a "Come hither, I'm almost
dead" seductiveness. I contemplate the hyperactive little Puer-
to Rican who stations himself at the pay phone and happily jab-
bers away for hours at what, I've long suspected, may be a dial
tone. I study the antics of the cocaine cuties and their ricochet
dashes to the toilet stalls. I watch the shy boys who pretend social interaction by tapping their fingers and nodding their heads
to the music, as if they're here for the sound track instead of the
movie. And finally, I watch for that nearly extinct breed at incestuous neighborhood bars: New Faces.

New Faces come without histories or connections or names.
They're fresh meat in an otherwise leftover buffet. But they
have to be careful. One visit too many and a New Face becomes an Old Face faster than the snap of a Heineken flip-top.
I've seen it happen. In the mirror.

So it's to my great astonishment that I encounter an entirely new species. A New Face that's actually an Old Face.

I'm seated on my bar stool, directly in front of the mirror. But
my reflection is standing? I stare long and hard at myself, and I
suddenly realize I have two images in the glass. In two different
shirts. One is a sleeves-rolled-up polyester, the other is a break-
the-bank Versace raiment. In addition to the Versace, Standing
Me sports a haircut that probably has its own movie career. I
conclude that if this is some kind of schizophrenic delusion, my
splinter image is living pretty damned high on the hog.

I'm rather taken with myself. I like the way I look. Despite
the fact that I am not now nor have I ever been my type.

What the hell is going on here?

Standing Me gives Sitting Me a broad, incautious smile followed by a cocky wink. Sitting Me flirts back with a nervous

tic that resembles the prelude to a grand mal seizure.
By now it's apparent, even to socially comatose Sitting Me,
that there are two different people here. We just happen to
look precisely alike. In the way that before and after photos
look alike—same features, different style.
He leans toward me, and my heart clenches. The last time a
stranger spoke to me in a bar, he asked me to get my foot off his
dangling scarf. But this glossy twin means business. A real conversation. I try to work up enough saliva to unstick my teeth.
"Do I know you?" he asks.
This is a trick question. What he's really saying is that his life
is so full and glamorous that he knows people he doesn't remember knowing. If I say yes, it means I'm a little creep who
remembers everybody because my life is so empty. If I say no,
he might take that as a kiss-off. I'm in a bind.
"Well," I answer, "you kind of look familiar." A neutral,
beige response that doesn't get us anywhere but doesn't end
the game either.
"Maybe that's it," he says nicely enough. "You just look like
somebody."
You, you big idiot!
"You ever get 'Matthew Broderick?'" he asks.
"Funny you should say that. No, never."
He laughs. Gorgeous teeth all the way back. "What are you
drinking?"
"No, what are *you* drinking?"
"Come on," he says, "I asked first."
"Yeah, but you were nice enough to think you knew me."
What the hell am I saying?
"What?"
"Nothing. Amstel Lite."
He leans over me to get the bartender's attention. I sniff one

of those colognes that comes in *Vanity Fair*. I suspect he applies
it from a bottle and not the page. "Two Stoli stingers." He
gives me a killer grin. "Trust me."

The last time I had a vodka stinger, I got tossed out of a sidewalk cafe. I was fiddling with the umbrella on my table, and it
came undone and toppled onto a stunned party of six retirees.
We clink glasses. "Here's looking at you," he says.

"Skoal," I answer. *Skoal?* I've never said *Skoal* in my life.

Half an hour later I'm licking the inside rim of my third
empty glass like a drunken raccoon. "Dee-licious," I slur.

"Mmmm," he slurs back. "Less go, OK?" He rises up, his
posture remarkably intact. "OK, less go." He pulls me by the
arm. I plant my numbed feet on the floor and walk toward the
door as if wading through knee-deep tapioca. Still, our sloshy
exit doesn't warrant so much as a sidelong glance. At the Candle those are reserved for exits on all fours.

The hurtling cab to Anthony's east-side apartment gives me
vertigo. I grit my teeth and reswallow what could potentially
be a date-killing projectile spew. It's a blur from cab to sidewalk to lobby to elevator to buttery leather couch. Anthony
finds the wherewithal to light candles, the only tolerable illu-
mination at this point. I ask for ice water and take a deep slug
of straight vodka.

"Jesus!" I gasp.

"Only live once," he mumbles.

"If I'm lucky."

He plops down next to me, and the cushion makes an elegant fart. "So, less hear all about Jim," he says as his manicured
hand explores my numb right thigh. His tone suggests the last
thing he wants to hear is anything about me.

"Who's that?" I point to a silver-framed photograph on the
glass-and-steel Parsons table.

Without turning, Anthony waves dismissively. "Nobody."

"That's one gorgeous nobody."

"Yup. All gone." He sighs and rests his *head* on my numb *left* thigh. As I run my hand through his Hollywood hair, I suddenly feel ominous furrows of scar tissue on his scalp. My fingers stop in their tracks, and I hope I haven't given my horror away. Anthony seems not to notice.

The worst part of me wants to leap off the couch and run screaming out the front door. The rest of me wants to know what happened to this man who, just a moment before, had been my flawless twin. I attempt a light mood, a bit of humor weighing in at about four tons. "So, you're probably wondering what brought me here tonight!"

"Nope."

"Well, Anthony, I'll tell ya. I never met anybody who looked so much like me before. I mean, didn't you notice? First time I saw you at the bar, I...I mean, you're much better looking, but..."

"*Much*," he says coldly.

"Ouch."

"Sorry, but I am."

"Hey, the truth is the truth." I'm surprised by how deeply hurt I am.

"So, Jim, whattaya do?"

"Little of this, little of that." I don't feel like talking anymore. "You?"

"Nothing."

"Your daddy's rich, and your mama's good-looking..." I whisper-sing.

Anthony sits up abruptly with a laugh. He takes a slug from my glass and improvises his own lyric. "And it's just my luck to get hit by a truck...."

"You serious?"

He finishes the vodka. "Half way to Sacramento, two in the morning. Good old Route 5 fog bank. Pow! Big old Kaiser truck right up my ass. Big old shit sound asleep at the wheel. Big old fuckin' settlement. And here I am." He points to the photograph. Jesus, I know what's coming. "And there I was."

If this were a play, the curtain would fall now. Anthony has the last line. I have nothing to say. I make sympathetic noises and reach out to him. This is consolation, not sex. He knows it.

"You don't want to see the rest of me."

"Anthony, come on…"

"I'm tellin' you, you really don't."

He stumbles with unusual grace toward the bar. I realize for the first time he has a limp. He catches my eye in the mirrored panel. "Whattaya drinking?"

I walk to him. "Do I at least get a kiss?"

We're both standing in front of the mirror now. I give his reflection the best smile I can come up with. "Well, hey, they did a terrific job with your face. I mean, what a face!"

"I'm thinking of suing that fucker too," he deadpans.

I get the joke. And the hurt behind it. I want to leave, but I can't. Not just yet.

We raise our glasses in the mirror. This time without the clink.

"Salud."

"Here's looking at me," I say.

A Turkey Bar Plucking
by Dean Durber

I was in Fukuoka for a three-day business conference. Endless boring speeches on money, commodity, and the process of transaction. But business was the last thing on my mind.

Before leaving home a friend had told me about a place called the "Turkey Bar." That was his literal English translation of the sign on the door, but most people, he said, referred to it by another name. He refused to tell me what that was. He said it was something I would have to discover for myself. He also said that if I wanted to see the most gorgeous Japanese boy alive, more beautiful than I could ever possibly imagine, I should go there. So I went.

"Irasshaimase," I heard, the Japanese way for a host and his gang of boys to bring attention to the fact that a new customer has entered the bar and to welcome that customer inside.

I was one of but six customers, and the only white one. Three barmen crowded behind the counter in an establishment that had room for no more than ten drinkers at a push. Intimacy and a heap of personal attention were the Turkey Bar's biggest draws. I sat at my assigned position, with a spare stool between me and the man next door. The master of the place left nothing to chance. This was not a bar for freedom of conversation. Nor could I just pick out the guy I wanted and do my own chasing. Nothing took place here without direct consultation with and the explicit permission of the man in control. If anybody sat in the empty seat beside me, it would be because the master approved of their interest in either me or the man to my left. That's the Japanese way.

I spotted the boy at once. By far the cutest, smoothest barman that has ever walked the earth. And for someone who has not exactly led a sheltered life of sexual pleasure, that's saying a lot. My friend had not failed me, except that his detailed description of the boy's physique did not do him justice. Nothing could have. You can't call a boy of such beauty a god without doing insult to looks far too exquisite even for heaven.

I wanted that boy. I wanted him now. But there was one minor problem. He, Juichiro, was unavailable. No questions asked. Rules of the job: A barman shall never engage in sexual relationships with a customer of the establishment. And besides, my friend had told me that he wasn't into *gaijin,* as the Japanese call foreigners.

I accepted a hot towel from Juichiro's gentle hands and wiped my sweaty face. It was humid outside but cooler indoors. And yet strangely hotter. I ordered a beer—Kirin lager poured from a tiny brown bottle with a massive price tag. Every song on the karaoke box cost 100 yen. I was given snacks to nibble on and a jumbo packet of Mild Seven cigarettes, compulsory, paid for even if not eaten or smoked. Plus, I knew, if I hoped to go home with Juichiro, I would have to insist that he join me in drinking—at my expense. It was going to be an expensive night.

Juichiro constantly looked my way, hardly surprising considering I was a fast drinker and needed the constant attention of his hands to refill my glass. And then his own. I noticed his

furtive glances even more so because my own gaze was permanently locked upon him, watching him wherever he went,
up and down the bar. I missed him every second he spent in
the kitchen, out of view. I drooled each time he raised his
elbow to pour beer, admiring the shadowy patches of black
hair that sneaked from the crevices of his armpits. Brown,
smooth skin touched only by a chain of gold that hung around
his neck. And those eyes. God those eyes. But how was I to
approach him? The bar was too small for discretion. My Japanese writing skills were minimal. I could probably manage to
slip him the phone number of my hotel, but I didn't want to
wait for his call. I needed him tonight.

"Join me in a song, Juichiro?"

Applause from all around. The foreigner was about to sing
the only song he knew in Japanese: "Kokoro, My Heart."

Standing on the tiny stage erected in a corner of the room
for kings of the karaoke machine, Juichiro and I shared the microphone and stared ahead at the television screen displaying
the lyrics to the song. I could not make head nor tail of the
printed words, so I was glad to have known most of this one
by heart. Juichiro charmingly filled in the gaps when necessary.
I used the excuse of having only one microphone to get my
lips as close to his as I possibly could. I didn't want to make it
too obvious, but for one tiny second, one tiny fraction of a second, I felt the touch of his tongue on my bottom lip. And suddenly the song came to life, bringing meaning to every word—
"My breaking heart yearns for you my love, as tender as a
rose"—until the music died.

"You wanna fuck?" he asked.

The mike was still on, and everybody in the bar understood
that little bit of English. They applauded even more. It was a
public proposal which could not be turned down for fear of

bringing huge embarrassment to the one who'd asked for such favors.

"Sure."

As casual as could be, I bowed to my audience.

"Let's go then."

To think I had listened to my friend when he said there was no way the master would allow this boy to go home with a customer. To think I had worried that the color of my skin was not to Juichiro's liking.

I went back to my stool to pick up my tab and pay the bill.

"Where are you going?" asked the master. "It's not over yet."

I laughed with him, a hungry laugh that conveyed my gratitude for such an enjoyable time. But I was now more than happy to call it a night. I was going home with the most gorgeous boy in the land. Where was he now? I wondered. Taking his time out back getting his things together, I thought, until he reappeared wearing nothing but a semi hard-on.

The men in the bar cheered. One of them obeyed the master's order to lock the door.

I had a decision to make. Either I could get up and perform for these men and do myself a huge favor in the process, or I could bail out and never show my face there again. It was not a difficult decision.

I had always wondered whether nerves created erection problems for porn stars in front of all those beady-eyed cameras. This, I decided, was payback time for the hours of torture I had subjected those guys to, just to fulfill my own obsession with voyeuristic pleasure. The cameras were now turned on me. But the aching in my trousers told me my nerves weren't going to be a problem.

I soon guessed this was not the first time such a show had taken place. The bar was well-equipped with condoms and lube. A change of lighting and sound altered the mood, and an air mattress was placed on the stage by the master of the house. I gulped a glass of beer and removed my clothes under a spotlight, receiving a thunderous cheer as my underpants slipped past the cheeks of my arse.

Juichiro was waiting, playing with his cock. He spread his arms to welcome me. The bar grew quiet, and I soon forgot about the voyeurs. The only sounds were the gentle melody of music and the slurp, slurp, slurp of my dream come true.

Juichiro's skin was so smooth. I explored his hairless body, searching for signs of pleasure—his and mine. It was only when we started to fuck that our breath became audible—steamy hot vapors filling the room, the screams of a boy who made me feel as if I was the only one. And then we were surrounded by applause once more as we collapsed in a pool of sweat on the stage, and the lights came up to show us the satisfied faces of our audience.

I paid my bill. It included a substantial charge for the services I had provided. I hoped that most of it went to Juichiro. He deserved it. And now I recommend that place to anyone who happens to be going that way. Just ask for the Turkey Bar, or, as my friend later admitted, the Happy Cock.

No-Fun Club Kid Turns 30
by Mark Macdonald

I loved him so much, I couldn't bring myself to tell him about the man who fucked me. When he told me about the man who fucked him, I laughed the same way I laughed when you told me you were dying—a callous, hard laugh. *Isn't life bumpy on the way down?* It was funny in a serious way. I told him I wasn't jealous, that I just wanted to know the score so I could orient myself now that Everything Changed. I thought of you: Didn't you say the same thing to your doctor? "Look, I'm not upset. Just tell me the gory details. I think I want to know."

So he told me what I thought I wanted to hear, and we sat there silent in the thundering throb of the stale disco air, glancing at each other, down to our drinks. I began telling him about you, how it was before.

Standing at the edge of the floor, watching bodies gyrate between strobes, my cigarette burned a blister onto my nicotine finger. I went to the bathroom, everyone cooing and combing and fluffing in vain, and soaked my finger in tap water. I gazed into the urinal as it seemed to fill with blood and decided the drugs must really be kicking in. I grabbed another beer and melted into the crowd.

Over walked Ryan, the cute blond boy who claims he's 16.

Everyone in there wanted him, he said, because he's tight and hairless—a real cutlet of chicken. But don't think he doesn't know how to use his assets. "Why don't you turn out to be really nice and take me home?" An impressive display to be sure. A hard-sell sales pitch of sin. But honestly, isn't this a school night? There I was, depressed and lonely, vulnerable to the advances of an angelic 16-year-old, but the drug-paranoia/jailbait thing set in, and I was gone in a flash.

Can't say as I blamed him for trying. There's a quiet, relaxed tension pulling stares in the chicken racket. Once I was able to do the same. You wander into some denim-and-cigar bar with unnaturally bad music and beer. You saunter, self-important, over to the bar for your labeled drink, in the hopes of cashing in without actually having to converse with these types. Sad, sadistic waves of your hand dismiss each of their valiant efforts, and they shrink back to their corner seats like toothless lions, predators no more. I did this kind of evil troll tour once a week and only ever felt guilty when I could no longer attract attention.

I was in the club with an attractive young friend, one of many at the time, and suddenly the crowd was too much, and I lost him. I wandered around drunk, searching for him, bouncing like a pinball between smiles and sneers, hair, boots, shirts, nipples, and garters. He had moved into the crowd somewhere, and for a minute I was stuck holding two beers. Interested parties see this and drop their pursuits like dirty needles. So this cropped, military type walked over and offered to take one of my two idiotic beers from me. I drank and smoked with him, this Bert or Bart or Kurt, who just moved here from Glace Bay, where they really know how to have a good time. "What's wrong with this place anyway? The people are so boring."

I ditched my beer somewhere discrete and followed him, this Herb or Martin or Grant, onto the dance floor. Right away he started making a scene, flailing about, all spastic, and he began instructing me step by step on how to dance erotic. He started grabbing himself like he didn't notice the alternative all around him, slowly backing away, and he closed his eyes and went into a trance or something, practically jerking off on the floor. After a while of this spectacle, I got bored and returned to my beer, which someone had swiped by that time.

How do *you* remember all this? Cold and burnt out like the bulb in the bathroom. Were you ever turned on? I find now that time is measured by these impulsive binges and half-blurred memories like dreams more than anything. You know, everything's fuzzy until you recount it for numerous people, witnesses give their versions, and you actually see the lurid photos some asshole took that night. Stories stretch like a wake behind a boat, becoming less memorable as you top them with new extremes, as if each justifies the whole. More shocking, more stupid, more embarrassing: anecdotes that cover past plateaus like a rake over sand. The high points get higher, the low points get lower. Each evening must reach this surreal climax, when everything clicks, and you realize what an ass you're making of yourself or with which creepy individual you are about to fuck.

So, anyway, I was telling him about you. I tell them all, if they give me enough time and liquor. About how I went to the hustler bar and saw all of your ghosts. How I saw you at the leather bar, laughing, your eyes darting smartly up and down each man's denim. How I saw you at the pickup joint, rolling those bright coke eyes, with some new friend, coating your mustache in the foam of too many cheap beers. You partied hard with your friends and lovers and drifted from table to table like a shadow. I thought maybe you had sat where I sat, flirted with that over-friendly barman, the one who holds your hand as he returns your change. I saw you everywhere and knew you weren't there anymore, and I had to leave.

I told him about the party we had the night before you returned to the wide, fag-bashing prairies. Your stepmum and nephews and their lovers were there, and your friend told me he had to go home too. Everyone pretended to be happy, and no one mentioned you both were dying. The conversation didn't need to happen, you know; the things left unsaid always the most important. At your stepmother's suggestion we played a gambling game with dice, unspeakably inappropriate to play a game of chance but happily ignored. You had been gone for months when I broke up with your nephew and started cruising your old haunts. Did you know he's into women now?

You would always turn up in the background of these places, the bars, the restaurants. I told myself it was your illness I kept seeing, the subliminal scar burned into the faces of the ones left behind. Why didn't I go to these places when you were still here? It's like inheriting this whole fucking scene from a relative of no relation, a friend I never really knew, and all with this giant warning: Don't drink too much. Don't go home with strangers. Don't take risks. Don't let the bar scene become your life. I've done all of these things now, and I can't remember what it was like before I came out.

I left another bar with another friend, staggering, sweat-soaked and exhausted, scarlet with liquor and innuendo, arm-in-arm into the chilly night. Walking up the alley, we met a between-clubs drag queen in this monstrous brown-and-orange fake-fur gown, named Storm Warning: She leaves you wanting more. We sat with her and shared a joint. She told us about her outfit with the pushy air of a used car salesman and sang *Blues in the Night* all the way through. "No charge," she said, and trundled away.

I'm sitting with my boy, happy, committed, but still making eyes at passers-by. Suddenly I feel totally calm. This entire experience, the whole, tiny club world, is so familiar yet so surprising. It's like a cross between a freak show and a family reunion. This is the life. Surely, given the chance, we would all die young under the liquor and drugs and genital luxuries we find here.

What a way to go.

But now that the inheritance has been claimed, I no longer see your ghosts. Bar by bar, club by club, each theater, each West End apartment is slowly filling with my own ghosts. Each weekend returns with the familiar drunken laughter of the generation that filled in for your absence. Now that my world is small enough to fit into an evening, now that you have finally been exorcised completely, everything seems manageable. I will not write to you again, so rest well. The scenery has been changed and the next act beckons.

Patron of the Arts
by Jack Fritscher

A hustler bar is not, per se, "gay." There are hustlers. There are johns. Neither leads a particularly urban-gay lifestyle. Rough-trade tricks are essentially straight. Johns are essentially out of the gay circuit, often young, and not necessarily rich. Neither cares much for the gay bars of West Hollywood, the Castro, or Greenwich Village. The johns prefer lower-class "straight" males who don't fuck up sex with sentiment. The hustlers prefer not men but money. Sex is an easy means to cold, hard cash. In a gay bar the reciprocity is sex for sex. In a hustler bar it's sex for money.

So there I sat, in Los Angeles, in a hustler bar, on a stool near the jukebox. I had to remember that the johns, many of whom were more attractive than the hustlers, weren't looking for mutual gay sex. They were looking for a "straight" guy to fuck them silly. The only mutual satisfaction would derive from the exchange of money—some guys have a need for cash, some guys have a need to pay. Probably it all has to do with toilet training. Or something.

The lower classes are eternally attractive to the middle and upper classes. (Ask Pasolini, the martyred patron saint of rough trade.) Even with heterosexuals, every class knows what it's for. So there in L.A., I stood, leaned, sat, paced, smiled, watched, cruised with 50 bucks hot in my jeans, begging to pay, eager to cross the line and know what the fuck it felt like to buy my way into the low life of a street-smart, talk-show–trash hustler.

Rough-trade tricks are born in trailer parks in the American south, raised in foster homes, tattooed in juvenile facilities, saddled with one or two young sons by one or two 15-year-old bitches, and educated in prison, where the one important lesson they learn is, gay men are an easy mark.

Still, I felt confident: A john never fears rejection because all he has to do is flash more money at the young and dangerous, turning them into the young and willing. No matter what sex trip a john wants—S/M, water sports, dirty feet—it can be had. The kind of primal sex once found in rest stops, YMCAs, bus stations, and carnival midways with mechanics, sailors, hitchhikers, and gypsy men with dirty fingernails can now be found only in hustler bars. A hustler bar is as close as a man can get to sex with satisfaction guaranteed. Hustlers, in fact, invariably "guarantee you, man, we'll have a good time."

Rough-trade hustlers, in their wonderful anonymity and danger and wild taste, should not be confused with the slick, urban-gay hustlers who advertise through the classifieds in gay papers and for whom "muscle sex" is a stylized Kabuki ritual. Gay hustlers are high concept. Rough trade is just plain what it is.

Twenty-five bucks, average, gets a john a hustler for the first time: no frills, just laid-back trade getting his dick sucked until the john comes. A return bout costs less. Prices vary depending on the time of night, the night of the week, the proportion of johns to hustlers, and the specifics of the sex trip. Frequently, cab fare or a tip of about 10 bucks is tacked on when the "boy" has done his best at turning out a good performance.

The essence of hustling, after all, is show biz. And a taxi to a hustler is a status symbol equal to a limo.

It was Friday evening becoming Friday night on a full moon weekend in L.A., and the two camps, hustlers and johns, sported with each other like Montagues and Capulets. A tattooed, well-built, blond, goateed hustler with a buzz cut eyed my table and headed to the oldies jukebox. He played "I Don't Want to Walk Without You." I stood and moved near to him, a quarter in my sweaty hand, and scanned the selections for a musical reply. My choice: "Hit Me With Your Best Shot." We listened to the music, eyeing each other. Who was the matador? Who was the bull? He was more wary than I. "You wanna beer?" I asked.

"Yeah," he answered. "Bud."

At the bar a john leaned over to me. "That one," he said, pointing at the blond goatee leaning his butt against the jukebox, "will do it for 20 bucks. He's raunchy. Likes to get blown and have his ass eaten. He's quiet. Believe me, I know. He's a bit player in B movies. Action-adventure flicks. I've licked all those tattoos on his arms. I sucked on him for maybe an hour and jerked myself off till he pushed me back, sat on my face, and twisted my tits till I came. Yeah, 20 bucks. He's marked you."

I bought two Buds, brought them to the hunky hustler, who looked like a street-version cross between all of the Butthole Surfers and the terrific Henry Rollins. His eyes were electric sky-blue. With the cold beers in my hand, I felt like a straight guy away at a convention buying a drink for a B-girl. I began to have a Frasier-and-Niles kind of moral dilemma. I had no trouble with sex separate from money or money separate from sex. But, my god, sex and money combined… I thought of the stereotype that johns are old and ugly and degenerate. I'm not old or ugly. But the degeneracy of paying for sex squatted awkwardly on my head.

I remembered what my buddy, Old Reliable, a video artist

who lives to love hustlers, had said to me earlier in the evening: "Hustlers are actors. You're the producer. You've got the money. You're also the director. Hustlers will do as little as they can unless you direct them. Pose! Flex! Beat your meat! Let me suck your dick! Sit on my face! Spit on my face! Shit on my face! The price can go up. Don't come off cheap. Offer $40 for openers. If you hit it off, if you want more than to suck him off while he kicks back and smokes, if you want him to rough you up a little bit, add 10 bucks. You want him to pose for some Polaroids, add another 15. You want to shoot some video, add 30. You want him to sleep over, add 10. You want him to cuddle, add 5—and breakfast. And tip him by giving him a pair of your clean socks.

"This is Hollywood. It's a circus. But at least it's the big top. All the movie stars and TV people hire hustlers. Judy Garland loved rough-trade boys. Rock Hudson loved pay-for-play tricks. Stars pay for performances because they are paid for performances. Hollywood is where America brings its dreams. You can hire your fantasy. The world's great performances aren't on-screen. Great performances take place in the sack."

So I handed Blue Eyes With Buzz Cut his Budweiser, wanting to proposition him. But I couldn't. Shy or sly, he wasn't helping. Why did I have to pull the quiet type? I went out prepared, with cold cash, ready to be nasty, to go slumming, to fucking buy sex! How un-American to suddenly become a reluctant consumer.

I felt the power in my pocket—the cash. I thought, *Show him the money!*

Blue Eyes With Buzz Cut was hot as a July street in Venice Beach, the kind of sweaty macho clean achieved only by living out of a knapsack and brushing your teeth at an IHOP. Just my speed. In a post-Judas minute I'd take him straight to the barroom toilet, shove him against a urinal, and do him. If only coins weren't changing hands.

Then good old lust, like cavalry riding over the ridge in the last reel, developed its own logic. I stared into his incredible eyes. *Hustling,* I rationalized, *is the world's oldest profession. Moral-religious trips can't reject thousands of years of sex-theater history.* I laughed at my puritanical head but took very seriously my hardening dick with no conscience. Buzz Cut swigged beer and stared hard at me. Inexplicably I said, "I want to exploit you."

"Cool."

"Fifty bucks?" I asked. *Fifty? Why did I say 50?* My subconscious was worried whether or not he'd like me. I forgot that rough trade doesn't give a fuck about me.

"You ain't a cop, are you?"

Flattered—God, I'm such a kveen!—I answer no.

"Show me the money." Hustlers are able to work out deals with a john in a heartbeat. "Let's go," he said, and we strolled out with the bar full of johns and hustlers watching our cool-as-shit exit.

That night Blue Eyes with Buzz Cut was what he has long been: a terrific piece of ass. That night I, for once, became what I had long had an attitude about: a john. I mean, a patron of the arts.

It was more than OK. It was hot! It was a perfect relationship. Pleasurable. Easy come. Easy go. No hassles. No baggage about his old lady, pregnant in some Motel 86 on Sunset Boulevard. No listening to some guy camping on about his Catholic school experience with ruler-wielding nuns. That night of my initiation into L.A. hustler bars proved the old adage: There's no business like show business.

Bully in a Bar
by Gregg Shapiro

The night started out like this: badly. I had agreed to meet some friends for dinner at a trendy restaurant in the city. My best friend, Jody, had won tickets to a comedy club called Laughing Stock, and that's where we were heading after we ate. Jody was really excited about seeing the headliner because he had a crush on him.

Rumor had it that the comedian was gay, and Jody thrived on exactly those things: rumors, comedy, and gay men. Jody had tried his hand at stand-up and failed; luckily he hadn't quit his day job managing a movie memorabilia store in Oak Park. The few times he did perform, we were there, all ten of us. His humor was kind of dark and probably insulted some people.

My favorite bit of his was a routine about the far-south suburbs of Chicago. He was born and raised in Wilmette, and somewhere in his upbringing a total dislike of anything south of the city had been instilled. I was from the north side and shared his feelings but couldn't match his intensity or wit.

He would start it by saying, "Do you know the worst thing about living in Chicago?" Then he'd pause, but not too long. He didn't want anyone to think his act involved audience participation. "Indiana," he'd say. Then he would annihilate the suburbs near the Illinois-Indiana border. "Harvey. Who the hell wants to live in a town named after a six-foot invisible rabbit? And what about Hazel Crest, a town dedicated to Shirley Booth and a tube of toothpaste? Do the residents of Joliet stand on their balconies calling out 'Romeoville, Romeoville, wherefore art thou Romeoville?'"

By that point I'd be doubled over in laughter, my eyes tearing. I'd heard the jokes so many times, I could almost recite them myself, but there was something in his delivery, a combination of maliciousness and affection.

Then he'd say, "If people from Homewood are Homewoodians, are people from Flossmoor Flossmorons? And don't get me started on Stinkney—I mean, Stickney—home of the sewage treatment plant. On a clear day you can see Cicero." And so on.

It was definitely local humor. Unfortunately the locals didn't take to it, and word got around that Jody was a comedian to avoid. That short chapter of his life ended, but he still makes me laugh, and I love him for it.

Jody also knew how to make me mad. His fascination with rumors—their creation, spread, and results—bordered on obsession. I could probably count on one hand the number of times he hadn't begun a conversation with, "Guess what I heard today?"

I had just finished cleaning the apartment—a Saturday ritual—when the phone rang. "OK," Jody said instead of hello, "here's the plan. We're meeting at Freddy's at 5:45. We can go in two cars since there's eight of us. Brian's not coming because he and Mitch had a fight, and he wants to stay home and sulk. Shane is probably going to meet us at the restaurant, but he's not sure if he's going to the comedy club. He said something about a full-moon party somewhere. Anyway, the attire is casual but not too. Got that?"

When I didn't answer, Jody forged ahead. "I met someone who knows Benny's agent. And he's agreed to get me a private audience with him."

"Benny?" I asked, regretting it the moment I said it.

"Where have you been? Kansas? Benny, the comedian we're going to see tonight. Benny the Boner? Snap out of it, kid. What's-his-name's not coming back. We're going out tonight, remember? To get your mind off him."

What's-his-name was Willie, my ex. We'd recently broken up after three years, and I was still a little blue. Jody had taken it upon himself to help me forget him but still had a long way to go.

"Besides, I saw him and his new beau last night at the Condom Nation party at Vortex, and they looked dreamy-happy."

"New beau? Gee, that was fast."

"Oh, come on, two weeks is not fast."

"I wonder how long he would have waited if I'd died instead of broken up with him. He probably wouldn't even have observed a proper mourning period."

"Black isn't his color. And besides, you said it yourself: You broke up with him."

It was true. I had initiated the breakup. But only because I thought Willie wanted it. And here I was, feeling lonely and depressed about something I was fully responsible for. Like seeing a brick wall and making the decision to try and drive through it instead of around. Hearing about Willie and someone else turned my mood sour.

"Tell me about him," I said. "No, don't. I don't want to know."

"Well," Jody said, "someone told me that he's a bike messenger in the Loop by day and a DJ in some leather club by night. From the looks of him, I'd believe it. The boy has serious Michelangelo features. Sculpted to the nines. And not a hair on his body. Someone told me he's naturally smooth, but I think—"

"Enough," I said, "I don't want to hear anymore."

"Wait. It gets better. They met through one of those computer bulletin boards. That's just like Willie, isn't it? Here we are, going out on the prowl publicly, and he's in front of his computer playing gay Nintendo. I heard he does his computer dating at work. But that could be just a rumor."

"Shut up, Jody. I mean it. I don't want to hear another word."

"Well, I...OK," he said, acquiescing. "None of this is fact, anyway. I mean, I saw them together—and I mean *together*—and I just assumed—"

"Count me out tonight," I said, certain that was the only way to end the conversation and get Jody's attention at the same time. Jody was uncharacteristically quiet. I could hear him breathing. We lingered for a few seconds in a cloud of silence. Just as I was about to hang up, Jody sneezed.

"Bless you," I said out of reflex.

"Thank you," he said, "although I'm not the one who needs to be blessed. Listen, I know you're going through a rough patch, and I'm just trying to make it easier."

"You can start by saying good-bye, then hanging up."

I should have stayed home, but I couldn't. I decided to check out Willie's new bike messenger/DJ. According to the local club directory, I had three leather bars to choose from. One was an old standard, moved to a new location. The other two were newer, in a different part of the city.

I dressed in faded 501's, a T-shirt, black motorcycle boots, and a black leather motorcycle jacket with lacing on the side. I'd never taken the leather "uniform" seriously; I didn't own a

motorcycle and had only ridden on one once, hanging onto
the driver as if he were a rock jutting out of a cliff I'd just fall-
en over. Leather was simply a costume, an outfit. A getup to
get off in.

I had thought Willie felt the same way when we bought our
matching jackets, but given his choice of new boyfriends, I
wondered if maybe I hadn't been mistaken.

I wasn't completely unprepared for the leather scene. For a
while, just after my breakup with Willie, I'd gotten a series of
dirty phone calls. The caller would breathe heavily and list the
things he wanted to do to me in his cellar, which he referred
to as his "dungeon."

The first time he called, I thought it was Willie, drunk or
possibly stoned, trying to reveal a side he'd kept hidden during
our relationship. So I encouraged him. I told him that I would
love to be shackled to the wall and force-fed kielbasa. That I
wouldn't mind playing with each item in his cornucopia of sex
toys and latex novelties. That I wouldn't have a problem vacu-
uming his apartment with my feet bound, hands handcuffed to
the Hoover. But that I would have to draw the line at rolling
around in molasses with his Great Dane and Rottweiler.

When I balked at the molasses and the dogs he said, "Hey,
wait a minute—is this Tony? Is this 555-1555?" And before I had
a chance to answer, he hung up. He hadn't called back since.

I drove around the block a couple of times when I got to
the bar, but there was no place to park. The neighborhood was
residential, a combination of Hispanics and Koreans and assorted Eastern European immigrants, and I wondered what
they thought about the men in black leather going in and out
of the corner bar across from Wendy's. Finally, I parked in the
Wendy's lot.

The bar was a vegetarian's nightmare: The patrons were

packed in like cattle herded for slaughter. I weaved my way
through, staying close to the wall, spray painted with designer
graffiti. Generic disco played so loudly that conversation was,
at best, limited. I turned a quick corner and entered the backroom. Two video screens showed leather porn, men with
overly muscled bodies tugging nipple rings, spanking, and
shooting gallons of come at the camera.

When I ordered a drink, I asked where the DJ sat. The bartender pointed to an elevated booth near the entrance to the
backroom. I paid for my beer and walked toward the DJ
booth. On the way a young man with bleached-blond hair,
wearing chaps, a harness, and a studded jock, smiled at me.
"Welcome to the geriatric ward," he said. "You look too
young to be back here."

"You too. Or else you hide your age well."

"I'm looking for a daddy. What's your excuse?"

"I'm looking for…a friend."

"What's his name?"

I paused. "I'm not sure."

"Well," he said, "if I run into him, I'll tell him you're looking for him."

"Thanks," I said, and walked away.

Everyone in the back room seemed to be staring at some
point in space just over my head or to the left or the right. A
friend once told me that eye contact with the wrong person in
a leather bar could lead to long hours of unexpected pain or
pleasure. No one met my gaze, so I felt fairly safe—like maybe
I'd stumbled into a Helmut Newton photo shoot: all bark, no
bite. *S/M,* I thought. *Stand and model.*

I eased my way to the DJ booth. A fat man in lederhosen
was at the turntable. He had a long black beard and no mustache. His left ear was dotted with rhinestone studs from the

lobe to the top. I remembered Jody's description. No match. Game over. Try again.

I finished my beer and left.

Outside, two police cars raced up Clark Street, blue lights flashing, sirens screaming. I decided to limit my beer consumption. I was in no mood to deal with Chicago's men in blue.

I drove to the Hot Tin Roof, finding a parking spot right in front. I took this as a sign that my luck was about to change.

Movement inside was limited to short sideways steps. If the first bar was a cattle car, this one was a sardine tin. With a different crowd—younger, more attractive, more hard-core. I couldn't tell if the men standing outside the open door to the bathroom were waiting to get in, watching, or just standing there for lack of a better place.

In the middle, where the pool table and coat check were, the room was less crowded. But not much. Muscled leathermen wielding pool cues circled the table as if it were that night's sex partner. Beer bottles lined the pool table's edge.

To say the back room was dark would be like saying Millie Bush was a pampered pet. A small video screen on the wall over the bar cast a thin blue glow. The only other light came from high-intensity bulbs in the ceiling turned down to the dimmest possible level without being completely off. I didn't see so much as feel my way to the first available open space against a wall.

Was this Willie's style? I wondered. Darker and more gloomy than the bars we frequented as a couple. The DJ's taste ran more towards industrial music than the fluffy dance songs Willie and I liked. Could this DJ be Willie's DJ?

The bar back squeezed by with a tub of dirty glasses.

"Hey," I yelled, "where's the DJ sit?"

"Don't ask me why he plays this shit," he said. "Why don't

you ask him yourself?" And then he walked away, hoisting the gray rubber tub over his head.

I decided to scout him out myself. I walked to the back end of the back room, where a group of men had squeezed themselves into the darkest part of the bar. At first I thought they were dancing. Then someone grabbed my wrist and directed it to his exposed dick. Still holding my wrist, he closed my hand around it. I could smell poppers. Another man lit a cigarette, and in the brief light I could see that everyone was involved in some sex act or another. I let go and walked as quickly as I could back to the front room of the bar.

I ordered a drink to calm my nerves. And then I saw him. Not the DJ, someone else. Someone I hadn't seen for a long time. Someone I'd never forget.

He didn't recognize me. I could tell by the way he stared vacantly past me. There was no glimmer of recognition or familiarity. Of course, I didn't look the same. I was taller and my hair was darker. My body was bulkier, solid after years at the gym— broad shoulders narrowing to a 31-inch waist. The tag on the back of my 501's read 36, but my inseam was really only 35.

He wore his hair the same: cut short on the sides and back, curly and full on top. His body was still the brick-solid mass it had been all through school. I remembered him towering over me throughout our youth, and now I had to look down a little to take him in. I looked into his eyes from halfway across the dimly lit bar and knew for sure it was him.

Those eyes, that vacant stare could only belong to one person: Basil Nichols. Basil Nichols, who with one blink of those empty eyes could turn half the boys on the playground into monsters and the other half into a quivering assemblage of jello. I'd been part of the jello half. Basil Nichols, feared by educators, clergymen, parents, laborers, and 89% of humanity.

Now, if you would have asked me what my greatest sexual fantasy was, I wouldn't have hesitated for a minute to tell you. For years I scoured the gay bars in search of childhood bullies. You know, the guys who had some magical insight into your future, the ones who helped to cement your role in society, the ones who knew all about you before even you knew all about you. In short, Basil Nichols.

I decided to play it cool and headed to the bar for a beer. "I'll have a Coors," I said to the bartender who was wearing a dyed black jockstrap.

When he brought my beer, I asked what Basil was drinking. "Black Russians," he said, "since he got here."

"Been here long?" I asked.

"Couple of hours," he said.

I gave him a 20.

"Keep them coming," I said.

I waited until Basil had gotten the drink I'd bought him, then sauntered over. A man with a Mohawk, wearing black bicycle shorts, no shirt, and a leather jacket, pushed past, heading for the backroom.

"Someone's in a hurry," I heard Basil say.

"He must be late for a very important date," I said facing him. He raised his glass. "Thanks."

"Don't mention it. And that's, 'Thanks, sir.'"

"Thanks, sir," he said, and downed the drink.

"Been in back?" I asked.

"Not my scene...sir."

"Oh, really? From the looks of you, you could have a good time back there."

"Yes and no, sir. I like one on one better."

Sure, I thought, without his gang of thugs he was a pussy. He turned to face me full front, adjusting his basket. "You live alone? Around here? Sir?"

"Not far," I said. "What about you?"

"A few blocks. I walked over."

"Live alone?"

"Me and my lizard."

Lizard? I thought. *Is Basil still playing word games?* Was his lizard a pet or a pet name for his dick?

"Does the lizard have a name?"

"Hector," he said, grinning a mouthful of perfect suburban teeth.

"You got a name?" I asked, fighting the urge to say it when he did.

"Basil, sir. Like the spice."

"Nice to meet you Basil." I extended a hand, cold from holding the beer. "You can call me...sir."

"The pleasure is mine, sir."

"It could be," I said, "if you play your cards right."

"I hope we're talking about something a little more exciting than bridge or Old Maid, sir."

"How are you at poker?" I asked.

"It depends on what I'm dealt, sir."

"I promise not to stack the deck," I said. *Not too badly,* I thought.

And then he moved closer, pulling me to him with an arm as quick and strong as a tentacle. We breathed into each other's faces, eyes locked. He was solid. His hand moved down my lower back to the seat of my jeans. He found one of the rips below the left back pocket and inserted his hand. He closed his mouth and breathed through his nose. His eyes were as brown and empty as his glass.

I didn't know what to do with my arms. He added pressure to his hand in my jeans and our crotches met, more or less, both hard and warm. I put my hands on his shoulders and squeezed. I stopped myself from putting them around his throat. *Plenty of time,* I thought.

"Take me home. Now, sir."

Basil lived on a street that was mostly single-family homes. His apartment building, in the middle of the block, stood out like an unhealthy tree in a forest. He lived in a garden apartment that was sparsely furnished: a futon, some stereo equipment, a Soloflex machine. There were dirty dishes in the sink. The hardwood floors looked like they'd just been swept. The television was on, volume turned down, and the light on his answering machine was flashing. A referee's shirt hung on a hook on the back of the front door.

"You a ref?" I asked, the first words either of us had spoken since we'd left the bar.

"Gym teacher," he said.

Of course, I almost said out loud. *Basil Nichols is in charge of training the next generation of jock bullies.*

"In the city?"

"No, sir. At the high school I graduated from, in the burbs."

I thought he had dropped out. I didn't remember him at graduation. It was probably because I had a crush on the valedictorian and had blocked out everything else from that day. As he answered my question, he undressed. I noticed a tub of lube and a box of Trojans on the floor next to the futon. He wasn't wearing anything under the black Levi's. I was still dressed, watching him, looking around the apartment.

He walked a few steps over to me and slid my jacket off, dropping it on the floor. I helped him lift the T-shirt over my head. He wrapped his arms around me, giving me a bear hug. My boots left the ground. He pressed his face into my chest. I could feel the stubble on his cheeks and chin. I grabbed his head, my fingers in his hair, and pulled back. His eyes seemed to have changed color, as if someone had turned on a light inside his head. He lowered me a bit, tried to kiss me, but I just pulled his head back, farther away.

We released each other. He got on his knees and popped the buttons on my jeans, sliding them down to my boots. He moved backward, still on his knees, toward the futon. We were separated only by the length of my hard-on. Basil eased himself onto his back. He reached under the edge of the futon and pulled out a pair of handcuffs.

"Please, sir, if you would do the honors."

This was going to be easier than I'd expected. At the head of the futon was a radiator, still cold in September. I raised his hands over his head, putting the right cuff on first, threading the chain through the radiator, then the left.

His legs and his torso were muscular but not grotesque. At some point he must have taken the time to develop his body beyond just bulk. His legs and chest were dusted with dark hair, his stomach bare and flat. He had an average-sized dick and low-hanging balls.

He rocked gently from side to side on the futon, as if there were a rhythm track playing in his head. And then he flipped over onto his stomach. He half stifled a grunt. The handcuffs must have been cutting into his wrists.

His ass, lit by late-night television, was hairless, smooth, and domed. He turned his head, breathing into his armpit.

"My legs, sir."

"They're nice," I said. "What about them?"

"Under the right corner of the futon, sir. There's some Velcro restraints. There are places to fasten them near where you're kneeling."

And there they were.

Basil spread his legs, pointed with his toes to where the restraints could be fastened on the futon.

"You do this yourself?" I asked.

"No, sir. A friend of mine did it. He did the same thing to his."

I unfastened the restraints and slid them over his feet and around his ankles. I started to tighten the left one.

"Make it tight. So I can't move too much."

"Oh, I intend to," I said, fighting the urge to giggle. When the restraints were around both ankles and fastened to the futon, I stood up. My knees cracked. I looked down at my erection—so hard it hurt. I shuffled over to the television, jeans around my calves. I picked up the remote control and began changing channels.

"What are you doing, sir?"

"I'm looking for the weather channel," I said.

"Please, sir, don't make me wait. I want it now. I've been very bad, and I need to be punished. You can punish me, can't you, sir?"

"That depends on how bad you've been," I said. "How bad have you been, Basil?"

"Real bad, sir. Worse than you can imagine."

"Oh, I don't know," I said, "I have a pretty vivid imagination. And a pretty good memory too."

"A pretty good memory, sir? I don't get it."

"Oh, you will."

There was an old Jerry Lewis and Dean Martin movie on. It looked like it had been colorized. Jerry Lewis was mugging for the camera. Dean Martin rolled his eyes. I turned off the TV.

"I don't remember you being at the graduation ceremonies, Basil. Didn't you drop out?"

"The graduation ceremonies?" he asked. His voice a little uncertain.

"Yeah, graduation. Class of '76. Remember? Red, white, and blue tassels?"

"I wasn't there," he said.

"I wasn't there, sir," I said.

"I wasn't there, sir," he echoed. "I was expelled. I wasn't allowed to participate. I had to repeat my senior year in the fall. Then I dropped out."

"You never graduated from high school, Basil?"

"I got my GED."

He started to rock slightly. If he wanted to turn over onto his back, he'd have a hard time. The Velcro restraints were tight. He'd have to roll, uncross his wrists, then cross his legs at an awkward angle.

I pulled my jeans up over my hard-on. I picked up my T-shirt and slipped it over my head. The leather jacket was still on the floor where we'd left it. I walked over to the side of the futon in the direction where Basil's head was turned.

"I graduated from high school," I said, "first try. If you had been at graduation, you would have known I was second in the class. I also graduated magna cum laude from college. I did those things despite you. In fact, I think I owe you a word of thanks. You managed to keep me off most playing fields and out of most social circles, so I had the time to study and get good grades, make the honor roll. So thank you."

"Who are you?" he asked, his voice poised between fear and excitement.

"Who are you, sir?" I snapped.

"Who the fuck are you," he responded, a new edge in his tone, "sir?"

"Names are not important," I said. "So don't even bother guessing. Let's just say I'm one of the many."

"Many?"

"Many victims. Recipients of Basil's 'flaming fist.' You remember the flaming fist, don't you, Basil?"

"Vaguely...sir," he said and hesitated. "Maybe you could refresh my memory."

"Yeah," I said, "you'd like that, wouldn't you?"

"Let me up," he said, "sir."

"You give, Basil? You giving up? And not a bruise or broken blood vessel or cracked rib on you. Not a scratch. Basil walks away unharmed again. The champ of the school yard."

"Let me up," he said again but louder.

I dropped to my knees, inches from his face. He flinched. "What's the matter, Basil? Scared I might hurt you. The night isn't long enough for me to hurt you the way you should be hurt. No, I'll be satisfied if I can just wound your ego. Leave a scar."

And then I grabbed his face with both hands and kissed him on the mouth. Our tongues jabbed at each other. My lips stung and I was afraid to check them, see if they'd been split. I couldn't taste blood, just alcohol. While I held his head, I turned mine, making sure to cover every inch of his mouth with mine. We both breathed loudly through our noses. The smacking noise echoed throughout the room. His eyes were open and I looked into them. They were moist. I tasted one of his tears as it rolled down his cheek onto mine and into our kiss. I stopped. His mouth was still open, not satisfied. A big hungry baby boy.

"Where's the key?" I asked.

"Key?"

"To the handcuffs."

"Top right-hand drawer in the kitchen."

I walked away from him. He was breathing hard, panting. I turned the light on in the kitchen. A cold, white fluorescent bulb buzzed over my head. I found the key and went back to Basil. He watched me approach, my face in shadow, lit from behind. I lifted the screen in the open window above the radiator. I threw the key out the window.

"What the fuck did you do that for?"

"Payback is a bitch," I said. "In a few days you'll probably lose enough weight to slip right out of those."

I walked into the kitchen and turned off the light. Back in the living room, I turned off the answering machine. Basil watched me and then dropped his head between his extended arms. He cried softly into the futon.

"Don't cry, Basil." I said, "Only sissies cry. Isn't that what you used to tell me? Take it like a man, and all that bullshit. What would the guys in the bar or the boys on the wrestling team think?"

His shoulders shook. I was surprisingly aroused. I could have dropped my pants and fucked him right there. It was a real Kodak moment. I took a picture in my mind, framed it, and put it on the mantle. I call it "Blubbering Bully."

Post-Communist Bar Trilogy
by Ernest McLeod

One: Our Pilot

We enter the Angel Bar in Budapest, Hungary, and discover they are doing the numbers game. We have experienced this game twice before: once in Hawaii, once in Madrid. Everyone who wants to participate wears a large tag with a number on it, and there is a system in place for relaying messages to the numbers of your choice. In this case the system is a prominently placed bulletin board. In both Hawaii and Madrid, my lover and I had little success with the game, so we have few expectations.

Having few expectations seems to make us very alluring. Almost immediately my lover gets a wink from a cute, impish looking young man standing nearby. Noting the young man's number, my lover proceeds to the bulletin board where, lo and behold, there is a message saying—in Hungarian—"I'd like to get to know you better." The young man loiters in our vicinity, sneaking glances. My lover—who counts Hungarian among the several languages in which he is reasonably fluent—engages him in conversation.

His name is Zoltán, he says. He's 23 years old and works as an airline pilot.

"A pilot?" we ask, surprised and intrigued.

Meanwhile, our visiting American friend who has come with us to the Angel Bar is impressed with neither our new acquaintance nor the clientele in general. "A bunch of little disco queens," he sniffs, not hiding his preference for the more closeted, macho types we'd encountered at the thermal baths earlier in the day. He stands by, bored, as our pilot tells my lover about his recent flying experiences.

Yugoslavia was his last trip, he says, though precisely where in Yugoslavia he can't quite recall. Since this is 1995 and Yugoslavia no longer exists and there is a war on in what had once been Yugoslavia, this strikes us as odd, but we continue to listen. "I'm going there again on Monday," he says. "No, wait, on Monday I'm taking French lessons."

"French lessons?" we ask, confused. We also cannot help but notice that our pilot is more than a little jittery. He keeps shifting from one foot to the other and scratching at the fly of his jeans.

"What's going on down there?" our American friend asks undiplomatically, bluntly peering at our pilot's crotch.

"He says he has a headache," my lover translates, making us wonder about the boy's sense of direction. "He also says he's been here since five o'clock."

Five o'clock? Who goes to a disco at five o'clock? I did recall seeing our pilot when we first entered the bar—before he had become *our pilot*. I had taken note of him, not only because he was cute but also because he was sitting alone eating what appeared to be a hearty pork dinner. This was not an uncommon sight in Eastern Europe—young men sitting down to hearty pork dinners in the middle of a disco—but as someone more used to American gay bars, where eating meals is generally frowned upon, it still took me by surprise. *Maybe he's just had way too much pork and coffee,* I think, trying to give our fidgety friend the benefit of the doubt.

"Well, I've had enough of this," our American friend says dismissively, asking if we can arrange a cab to get him back to his hotel. In the process of seeing him out, we momentarily lose track of Zoltán. This is both disappointing and a relief: disappointing because I found his manner—fluctuating wildly between boldly flirtatious and shyly sensitive—strangely endearing, a relief because we are both beginning to suspect he may be ever so slightly insane. As he was speaking to my lover, I had simultaneous urges to pat his head reassuringly and to run while we still had the chance.

With our pilot off to parts unknown, we decide to dance. They're playing more disco than techno—fine by us since we've decided we're either too old for or simply don't get techno. The disco queens, as our American friend called them, are dressed up and looking good in our opinion. The energy on the dance floor is infectious and inclusive. We've been here before when the cold, slightly sterile atmosphere of the bar— too much money having been poured into it, I suspect, lending a contrived and desperate air to the poshness—made me feel foreign and self-conscious. But on this night the same elements put me in high spirits, as if we're one with the native crowd. We boogie to my favorite song of the moment, Billie Ray Martin's "Your Loving Arms," and then to the ubiquitous local hit "*Megtalállak még,*" by the Hungarian boy duo FLM. All the dancing boys know it by heart and sing along enthusiastically, as do we, having adopted it as our song too, the one that if we hear it 20 years from now will transport us immediately and nostalgically back to the fall of 1995, four months in Eastern Europe, there and gone in an instant.

Unlike the natives, generally significantly younger than us, our energy eventually flags, so we return to the cabaret upstairs where it's quieter and where there are tables and chairs. As we're settling in with new drinks, my lover spots Zoltán sitting by himself, hunkered over some food object. "What do you think he's eating now?" my lover asks.

"I think it's a whipped dessert!" I exclaim, watching our pilot jab a spoon into a tall glass parfait dish, the type you might see spinning around festively with a cherry on top behind chrome and glass in an all-American diner. He's concentrating on his confection so privately and intensely that it seems almost rude to watch him, as if we've caught him in the middle of a sexual act. So we sip our rum and tonics and focus our attention on the noneating clusters of boys around us. Young Hungarian men are a handsome lot, with their dark, gelled hair; brooding, dark eyes; and naturally toned bodies, the American gym obsession not yet having taken root in this neck of the woods. How refreshing, we think, to be in an urban gay setting where the young men don't look as if they've all been stamped from the same cookie-cutter. A few more years of hearty pork dinners, though, and the natural toning begins to loosen considerably.

The next time I turn to see what our pilot is up to, his table is empty, but I spot him moving purposefully toward some unknown destination with—whoa!—another whipped dessert. How many whipped desserts can one boy eat in an evening? Though I suppose the consumption of multiple puddings in a gay bar shouldn't in itself imply mental imbalance, it does again occur to us that our pilot might be just a tad, uh, eccentric.

After checking the bulletin board again, in vain, we return to the dance floor, where it doesn't take long for us to notice our pilot dancing and flirting with someone other than our-

selves. Maybe because we have received no other solicitations
in the numbers game or because our dim-witted male egos
can't stand the thought of any sort of rejection, however well-
advised, we decide to realert our pilot to our humble presence.
And like a puppy tempted by any vaguely new toy thrown in
its path, his attention wavers from his new friend back to us.

Our pilot's dance style is as erratic as the rest of his personality—the dance of a man on a major sugar rush. His favorite
move is to hang back at a great distance, then pounce very suddenly forward in our direction, vigorously waving his hands in
front of our faces, as if otherwise we might drift off to sleep on
him. After a while, his lurching makes me queasy, so I suggest
to my lover we adjourn to the semisecluded space a couple of
steps up from the dance floor. From this space both the dance
floor and the entrance to the dark room can be observed; it's
sort of the anteroom to the dark room. Zoltán follows.

Our pilot's hands wander lightly over my torso. He pulls
open my shirt and peeks inside to check the topography. He
seems especially infatuated with my neck, which, in my experience, isn't the first place men's hands wander. "He says we
have exceptionally young looking necks," my lover translates.
"Hands too." Since I can't recall anyone ever complimenting
me on my neck—even when it was exceptionally young—I
take this flattery to heart and allow our pilot to undo my buttons one by one. We adjourn to the dark room.

There we let our hands wander over our pilot. We block our
memories of his hands scratching at his crotch earlier in the
evening. It is very hot and very dark. After playing for ten or fifteen minutes, our pilot's sugar rush crashes big-time. He rests his
head on my chest, where it remains for so long, I fear he will
take up permanent residence. His full weight against my torso
becomes increasingly heavy. Body parts start to go to sleep. I tap

him on the shoulder. "I think we're going to take a little break."
My lover and I return to the anteroom where we refresh and
gather ourselves, making sure everything is zipped and tucked.
We expect that our pilot will follow, but he does not. We
wait. No sign of him. The dance floor is clearing out. If we
stay longer, we'll have to squint into the dawn to get home.
We're ready to call it a night.

Since we've had intimate relations of a sort, we think it
would only be polite to find our pilot and wish him bon voyage, wherever his next destination in life might be. We return
to the dark room. It's only bright enough to make out a few
vague shapes, but eventually we think we spot him in the form
of a person crouched forlornly on the floor, head between his
knees. Someone is kneeling beside him, offering comfort, we
assume. We linger in the shadows, trying to comprehend the
melodrama. Have we somehow upset our pilot? Or has the
sugar meltdown led to some inexplicable emotional distress?
We bend down next to him to see if we can be of assistance. I
put my hand on his shoulder. But wait—the texture of this
shirt's fabric is not familiar, not the fabric I'd slipped my hands
under earlier, not the fabric I'd felt against my chest. In the
dark you remember textures.

"It's not him," I whisper to my lover. "Oops, sorry," we
mumble, stumbling away in the shadows.

We comb every inch of the dark room. Zoltán isn't there.
Since, as far as we know, there is only one exit, our pilot's disappearance is kind of spooky. Logically, we assume he must
have slipped out without us noticing, or perhaps there is a secret exit we don't know about, one that only a select few are
privy to. Maybe he even works at the bar and gets free meals
here. Maybe he's never flown in a plane.

But we both long to believe his disappearance is more roman-

tic and mysterious than that—that, come Monday, our fearless
pilot might be entirely capable of touching down in a war-rav-
aged land before bounding off to his French lesson at a gay café
featuring all manner of deliciously decadent whipped desserts.

Two: Action

You walk down a dark side street in a foreign city and look
for the neon *A,* then enter, walking down from street level,
sort of like *Cheers,* only the people inside don't know your
name, and you can't just saunter in casually like Norm and
Cliff; you have to be buzzed in. By this time everyone near the
entrance has been alerted to your arrival, so you feel especially self-conscious and subject to inspection. You are with your
lover, and it is only your second night in this foreign city,
though you plan to stay for four months. From the name you
think you might know what kind of bar Action Bar is, but you
aren't completely sure. If it is the kind of bar you think it is,
you and your lover have worked this out, mostly: together
OK, separately not. Some people scrutinize you as the latch
clicks open; some don't or pretend not to. Which is worse?

Furniture is scarce. From what you can see, the place has
sort of a dungeon or prison aura—complete with heavy chains
attached to the walls. But since the walls are a warm brick and
the ceilings are nicely vaulted, a more elegant wine cellar also
comes to mind. You go to the bar, and you order wine, which
leads the bartender to kneel surreptitiously behind the counter
and position two giant tumblers beneath some kind of hidden
spouts. Mystery wine. *Uh-oh,* you think, *hangover big-time,* and
you're supposed to start looking for apartments tomorrow.
And you will be right about the hangover.

You drink your first giant tumbler of mystery wine and dare
to order another before venturing deeper into the bar. You act

like you're not interested in or already know why people are coming and going from a low, dark hallway, but actually this is distracting you from most other thoughts, so finally you say to your lover, "Shall we see?"

You go down the low, dark hallway, heads bent, and enter a room illuminated solely by the flicker of a video monitor. You glance at the video and try to figure out what your next move should be. Around the perimeter of the room is built-in seating, and toward the center are a couple of high tables around which people can lean. There are a few people sitting in the shadows, but you can't tell what they look like. No one is talking.

Concentrating deeply on not overturning your new brimming giant tumbler of wine, you select a spot on the built-in seating, which, since it's reminiscent of bleachers, makes you feel like you might be at a high school sporting event—except for the darkness and the solemnity and the fact that the event is three men fucking on the video screen and the real but unacknowledged sport is more like hunting than basketball. On-screen there's lots of thwacking and slapping, and even now—comfortable with your sexuality as you are—you are embarrassed to watch this with strangers in a deathly silent room.

These three men finish, and another video begins. This time it's an attractively wholesome-looking boy who, after an infinitely lengthy drive into the country, takes out a picnic basket and wanders into the woods. He unpacks his belongings, which include an enormous watermelon—it's all quite bucolic—and then unpacks himself from his clothes and begins to carve the watermelon, and you think, *Oh, my, is he really going to?* And he does, followed by even messier escapades involving whipped cream and smushed grapes. It's really more funny than erotic—really quite funny—and you would like to laugh,

but looking around at the other men in the room, you understand that laughing would not be cool at all. Hunting is an absurd yet extremely serious sport.

Every once in a while, you see out of the corner of your eye
figures loitering near and then disappearing through a doorway
(now clearer since your eyes have adjusted to the darkness) in
the back corner of the room. Disappearing into an even darker darkness. Sometimes they reemerge within seconds, nonchalantly, as if they just needed a quick stretch of the legs;
sometimes they're gone for a few minutes and reemerge a little flustered; sometimes they don't reemerge at all. You hear
the click of metal against metal, a soft groan, a loud sigh.
Though everyone is absolutely still, you feel tension zipping
around the room like an electrical current. Suddenly, several
people rise and vanish into the blackness, one after the other.
Your lover pokes you. You follow him. Sadly, everyone has
lost interest in the lone picnicking boy.

You keep hold of your lover's hand so at least you'll know
that when another hand finds some part of you, it is not his.
You really cannot see a thing. You wonder how far back the
darkness goes—forever, it seems—and feel an excitement akin,
you're guessing, to that of a cave explorer. Suddenly, a lighter
sparks the darkness but only long enough for you to register a
single, disembodied image. Another lighter sparks, another disembodied image. Another. Another. Face. Forearm. Wrist-
watch. Cock. Three-dimensional space has lost all meaning.
Images of isolated body parts jumble in your mind, fade, seem
not quite real. But then you feel a very real hand, not your
lover's hand, on your crotch, squeezing the goods like the old
ladies squeeze produce at the open-air market.

You remember suddenly and alarmingly that you are claus-
trophobic and feel the need to get out immediately. You yank

your lover's hand toward the light. You push your way out. You imagine fires. Getting trampled. You rush to the bleachers, sweating profusely. You wipe your brow with the back of your hand. The messy picnicking boy has presumably gone home for a shower.

This could be any gay bar—or any gay bar of a certain sort that happens to be running a video of a boy fucking a watermelon. Bar. Basement. Porn. Dark. The frenzied rustle of anonymous couplings on a busy night. On a slow night the sense that lifetimes are passing in the real world while you wait in vain for the next one, the perfect one, the marginally perfect one, to arrive. *Just five more minutes,* you say, and when those five minutes have elapsed, you say, *OK, just five more. Five more, that's it.* And then, like a miracle arriving the moment you are prepared to give up all hope, there he is, the perfect one, walking in right in front of you.

So different from these other desperate cave dwellers. Well-dressed, well-scrubbed, like he might actually have a life outside these walls. Of course, in this light it's hard to see him, but you pray he notices you, and he seems to. He doesn't loiter, doesn't sit nervously on the bleachers fingering his glass or watching a boy smush grapes against his nipples. He disappears into darkness with no shameful hesitation, confident you will follow. And you do.

You find him. He kisses you. He is hungry—hungrier than you expected someone who looks like him would be. You worry that your eyes were deceiving you. You feel his tongue exploring your mouth, lapping your ear. Yes, very hungry. Your index finger grazes his denimed thigh. You hope it's his tongue in your ear and not someone else's, though truthfully, in the absence of light, does it really matter? It comes down to feeling rather than aesthetics. As long as your mind imagines beauty, a tongue is a tongue is a tongue. You try to find your lover's hand again, for reassurance. You remember your earlier panic attack, that need to flee has killed other such encounters in the dark.

By now you realize there are others around you, pressing in like a greedy school of fish, ready to devour. The three of you press deeper into the darkness but the greedy school follows. Your lips search for his lips, trying to recapture that initial seizure of pleasure, trying to pretend this can still work. The stranger's lips pull away. This isn't going to work. The stranger whispers in your ear, in accented English, "We can go?" Yes, push them aside, leave those ugly cave dwellers behind.

And when you return to the light, it stops being any gay bar of a certain sort because suddenly you are faced with a real person, a person who has a real name, which he reveals to you— a common name here, like John or Mark, but one you would never encounter at home—and a real history, which he does not reveal to you, not yet at least. Even in this relatively bright light, he looks as good as you expected, better really. His facial structure is exquisite, his skin silky smooth, his eyes cool and sharp, his personality warm. You are thrilled with the relative ease and fine quality of your catch but anxious about what will happen next.

He suggests a taxi, going to his place, which happens to be in the most romantic and desirable part of town. It's a bit awkward now, this real person forcing you to make real decisions, and you feel the same bar patrons who scrutinized you when you arrived scrutinizing you again, knowing exactly what sort of transaction is taking place. You imagine them envious of your good fortune and like that idea. You hope they don't think it is necessary for you to buy this person's affection. You hope they don't know something you don't know. Perhaps they've watched this same transaction before, perhaps many times. Perhaps you're the fill-in-the-blank tourists, the American fag cliché. This idea you don't like, but since the taxi is waiting, there is little time to ponder. The stranger with a name motions, and you follow him into the night.

The taxi speeds through the strange streets of this foreign city, speeding so fast you feel like you're in an emergency vehicle, like this is an actual emergency, though a potentially fun one. You press your face to the window and see the lights of your foreign city flash deliriously, exhilaratingly by. You see lamplight in apartment windows and briefly wonder about the people inside. Briefly wonder how many of them are having sex or, like you, are about to have sex. In some ways this is the most exciting part, when the sex is all promise.

Soon the promise is cracked open, and your perfect stranger is, superficially at least, no longer a stranger. You see where he lives, how he lives: a half-finished glass of red wine beside the bathtub, a squeezed tube of toothpaste beside the sink, jeans and a T-shirt hung up to dry, sex toys pulled down from a shelf, carpet lint beneath a table. You undress him. You explore the terrain of his body, inch by inch.

You are not disappointed—quite the contrary—though you find your proclivities do not quite coincide. You even meet his dog, who nuzzles your hand affectionately and then retreats to her bed, casting appalled sidelong glances at those nasty humans at it once again. Afterward he asks if you want a sandwich and makes one for himself and eats it naked in the tiny bright kitchen. The dog, delighted that that *other* business is finally over, comes running. The first hints of your hangover blossom behind your eyes. You want only to sleep.

It is hardly an anonymous encounter. But as you kiss him good-bye, he's still a stranger. And, for the next four months, each time you see him in passing, at the baths or in another bar, he grows more and more distant, until it seems less and less likely that you ever met.

Three: Love

Another of those impossible to find places—dark side street off the tourists' path, no sign, improbable stairs to an unmarked basement door—that seem, the moment you enter, thoroughly unpromising. Inside, a typical neighborhood pub, not readily identifiable as gay until you spot tell-tale photographs and magazines. The crowd is a mixture of Poles and foreigners, with quite a few English speakers. The seats are all taken. But to honor our trouble, we decide to have one beer before we leave. Just as we're draining our glasses, a place clears on the bench running along one wall. Well, what the hell? One more—observe the crowd for a bit, absorb a little foreign gay culture, or if that's predictable, which it often is, browse through the quasipornographic magazine we picked up on the way in called *Men!*, also predictable but diverting nonetheless.

A few pages into *Men!* we are diverted from it by the arrival of a very drunk young man with a throbbing Walkman clamped to his head. He's disheveled and dirty, wearing one of those trademark baggy and shiny jogging outfits that hint at poverty and provincialism. He plunks himself down to one side of us and strikes up a conversation with another man sitting near us, pausing at one point to scream "Shut the fuck up!" at a rowdy corner table.

Then, out of the blue, he turns to my lover and says, "Are you gay?"

"Of course," my lover says, hardly willing to deny this fact in a gay bar.

The drunk boy scowls and cranks his Walkman even louder,

as if to blast all unwelcome thoughts and voices from his head. The man he had been talking to says to us, "He goes out and gets drunk and then comes here to find someone to make love to him. He has a car parked outside."

Whatever animosity I held towards this kid—along with the fear he might want to pick a fight—mutates into pity. He comes here full of rage and alcohol to find someone to make love to him! I wonder if he has any idea that whatever sex appeal he possesses has been drowned by alcohol and whatever stripping away of personality he has to undergo to get himself through the door. I wonder what kind of lovers he finds this way. The thought of him driving a car is horrifying. He sits silently next to us for a while, eardrum-splitting music still pummeling his brain, then stands unsteadily and staggers off to confront the rest of the bar.

Just after he leaves us, another young man enters, this one the very opposite of the drunk boy. He is strikingly tall and darkly handsome, dressed in clothes a bit formal for the bar— suit coat and black shirt, brown dress pants—but also clothes a student might wear. Everything about him is steady: his manner, his deep-set gaze, the deliberate way he takes off his suit coat and hangs it up on a peg. He orders a beer and, to our surprise, asks in Polish if he can sit with us. We discover he doesn't speak English—for which he apologizes—but that his Russian is fairly good, so he and my lover begin a conversation which, in turn, my lover translates for me. His name is Jarek, and he is in fact a student.

I keep tabs on the drunk boy during translation lags, watching first as each table, not surprisingly, chooses to ignore him, then as he sits alone, Walkman still audible over all barroom conversations, and then as he moves, even more unsteadily than before, to the staircase and partially up it, pausing, looking back—with what? longing, hatred of us, hatred of self, despair, disgust, all of the above?—half waving good-bye as he stumbles out of sight and presumably into his waiting car. No one tries to stop or save him. It is easier to pretend he doesn't exist, perhaps as he'd like to pretend this part of himself doesn't exist.

I turn my attention back to the conversation with Jarek. Though I can't understand him directly—a frustration I've faced often in our foreign travels—I'm immediately drawn to his earnestness and openness. I sense that he knows people in the bar—he entered with the air of someone who had been here before—but his attention is directed toward us. He discusses everything from the city in which he grew up, to Polish history, to gay life in Poland as he perceives it. He says he has seen *Priest,* which is drawing huge crowds and causing quite a controversy in Catholic Poland. As we have found when talking to other twenty-something Eastern European gay people, there is little talk of coming out, at least in the American sense. The discussions center more on broader issues; there is an eagerness to share with us something of their country's history, gay history as part of this perhaps, but rarely personal history. Perhaps because I'm missing the nuances of what Jarek is saying, or perhaps because the beer has begun to cloud my concentration, I find myself focusing more on the intensity of Jarek's voice and gestures than on the exact details of his remarks.

We sit and drink beer and exchange stories, and the rest of the bar slips away. There is only Jarek and us.

Until the intruder arrives. At first, American-visitor manners intact, we try hard to be polite. The intruder, on the plump side and sporting an unflattering ponytail, announces he's just had his 30th birthday. We congratulate him.

"Cheers," I say, raising my glass to his.

He looks appalled. "What is this *cheers*? No, I don't like it."

He flips through our copy of *Men!*, and as he turns each page he says, "Is *this* what you like? Is *this* what you like? Is *this* what you like?"

"No," we say with increasing irritation, afraid of losing Jarek's interest. "*This* is not what we like."

My patience runs thin, particularly when the intruder speaks to Jarek in Polish and my lover understands enough to know that he is basically saying, "Don't associate with these awful Americans." I have fantasies of smashing my heavy beer glass over his pudgy Polish head. Fortunately Jarek, the good Pole, is not swayed. He continues speaking to us and ignores the intruder until finally—yes!—the pest goes away.

I'm not sure when the line is crossed exactly, but at some point I think I'm in love with Jarek—or as in love with someone as you can trick yourself into being in the span of two hours. I wonder if I would be as smitten if he were an American or even speaking English. Probably not. But there is a genuine desire to know him, more so than with anyone else we have met on our trip, and as the evening continues, my desire to know him melds gradually, almost imperceptibly, into a desire to have him. I wonder if my lover feels this way too. I suspect he does but to a lesser degree. My infatuations run both cooler and hotter than his.

Jarek excuses himself to go to the bathroom. My lover and I look at each other. There is no debate. We know that Jarek has a boyfriend, lives with him even, a rarity for young gay men here. The boyfriend is away for a few days. As justification, I tell myself that the boyfriend sounds like a controlling bitch. According to Jarek, his lover says it is a total disgrace he hasn't learned English or traveled beyond Poland. His lover left a detailed three-page plan for Jarek to follow in his absence. (Jarek has accomplished nothing outlined in the plan—a good

sign, we think.) But my justification is flimsy. I'm happy that
Jarek has a boyfriend, but honestly, the fact that we will soon
be pressuring him to cheat on his lover doesn't really bother
me. I'm in a greedy mood. I want exclusive rights, if only for
one night.

Jarek returns from the bathroom. My lover delicately phrases in
Russian the question, "Would you like to visit our hotel room?"

I notice that now we are literally the only three people left
in the place. The bartenders are wiping tabletops and putting
chairs up. The evening has been endless and has passed in an
instant at the same time. Since up until now our talk with Jarek
has only touched on sexuality and has roamed nowhere near
actual sex acts, I'm prepared for him to quickly say no and be
offended at the suggestion, thinking, *So this is what the lechers
were after all along!* In fact, I can't even look at him as my lover
pops the question. In my mind a true but passionless sentence
like, *Sorry you can't join us, but it was a real pleasure to meet you
anyway,* is poised disconsolately for my lover's translation.

There is no need for it, however. "He didn't hesitate for a
second," my lover says.

I look Jarek's way again, barely able to contain my glee. The
broad smile on his otherwise serious face needs no translation
either. I realize he was prepared for our question and for the
answer he would give. Though many glasses of beer have been
consumed, he rises as steadily as he sat down, and once again
we wait for a cab to take us into uncharted territory.

And the drunk boy, I think as we get in the taxi, where did
his rage end up tonight? I hope he found someone to hold and
assuage it, temporarily at least. Then I hope someone else will
come along to shake him hard, jolt him from his misery and
hatred. Make him see that desire can be a gift instead of a curse.

In my experience, which is hardly vast, the best one-night

stands are the saddest. Even before we say good-bye to Jarek the next morning, I know I will be filled with an exquisitely sentimental melancholy, a melancholy that in this case my lover and I are able to share. I also know that as soon as I get a good night's sleep again, the exquisite sadness, like the sadness that accompanies the return home from a wonderful vacation, will fade, and so, however exhausted I am (very, since for some reason I am pathologically incapable of sleeping next to a new lover), I want to postpone sleep for as long as possible.

We almost were not *permitted* to make love to Jarek. When we arrived at the hotel and asked for our key, the sour woman behind the desk sternly told us there were to be no visitors at this hour. (Never mind that the sidewalk outside the hotel was lined with female prostitutes.) But he's our Polish cousin, and he won't stay long, we improvised, very unconvincingly. She was not moved. Depriving three men of their only chance in this lifetime to make love to one another did not, apparently, trouble her.

I gripped the cold marble banister of the sweeping red velvet–carpeted staircase leading from the plush lobby up towards our Spartan room and, for the second time that evening, held murderous thoughts. Did this morosely drab woman, this unhappy holdover from Communist times, when hotel guests were as appreciated as cockroaches, really think *she* had the right to prevent us from slipping under the sheets together? Apparently so.

We waited and persisted, persisted and waited. My hand continued to grip the cold marble banister. My mind continued to plot in a cold-blooded fashion. Finally, in what seems to be the solution for all not-quite post-Communist service clerks who no longer want to deal with you and surely not with any unspeakable love in which you might intend to engage, she huffed, and she puffed, and dismissing us with a wave of her hand from which our key dangled like a jewel, she returned to her never-ending, not-quite post-Communist stack of meaningless paperwork. We smiled at Jarek. With no one else around, it was easy to believe the red velvet carpet had been laid out precisely for boys like us. We wished the woman behind the desk a fond good-night and ascended.

Who Is Hansen Waiting For?
by Gene-Michael Higney

Night after night I sat in my usual booth and watched the long line of guys trying to pick up Hansen. Good-looking guys too—all hitters waiting to get up at bat, only to be struck out by Hansen's polite but firm refusals. Kind of funny, except for the time I struck out. But that was early in the game, and I learn my lessons quick.

Always have.

Still, I often had a twinge of regret seeing all that talent get passed up night after night. I wondered, along with I don't know how many others, what Hansen was waiting for.

Or whom.

Whoever it was, he hadn't shown up yet.

Hansen talked with lots of people. Danced with a few. Went home alone. What a waste of six-foot something of collegiate good looks.

From time to time hitters would get annoyed. After several noes in a row, the sore losers would clot together and share their gripes, kicking the tar out of Hansen's character, pointing out his effete snobbery.

Those sessions never lasted long; Hansen wasn't a snob. He seemed to even like people. He also seemed to be waiting for something. Or someone. Night after night.

And I watched him wait.

Oh, there are times when even an aging writer of books only obscure critics and blue-haired old men read gets lucky. I was nowhere near as picky as Hansen. But on those long evenings when I was *not* so lucky, when I sat in the bar—I'm politely termed a "regular"—and watched Hansen nurse his beers, talk to strangers and friends, and gaze at the door from time to time, I would let my feverish and underpaid imagination draw verbal pictures (the only kind I ever could draw) of who Hansen was waiting for.

A long lost lover, no doubt. Someone youthful, maybe blond, and definitely godlike. Someone from whom Hansen was tragically parted and for whom he now waited in silent though attractive anguish.

Or maybe not.

A woman? A sister maybe? A mother? A girlfriend? Not he. Hansen was definitely a man's man. A twin brother? Separated at birth and driven by a nagging sense of incompleteness to find his "other"? Was there, somewhere out there, in some copy of this bar, a copy of Hansen politely dispensing maddening noes to rows of admirers while watching the door?

OK, maybe not.

I took the time, one very slow winter's night, to discuss Hansen with Nappy, a black queen who waitressed in the watering hole that had become my home away from homeless. And Hansen's too, seemed like.

Nappy was a little bitchy at first, having been rebuffed by Hansen several times, but after a while he gave me something to go on.

"Something to go on." That's how they talk in those tacky (but commercial) detective novels I hate so much because I can't write one.

Nappy told me about the night everybody thought Hansen was finally going to leave with someone.

The someone was even better-looking than Hansen, if Nappy is to be believed. The someone had been rather shy. Maybe his first time out in a bar. He and Hansen had spent hours in a booth, talking. Intent. Quietly involved.

It drove everyone in the bar crazy with delight and envy to see them—beauty times two—engrossed in one another.

Nappy, of course, did his damnedest to get near enough for long enough to hear what they were talking about. The regulars were *furious* with him when the ruse didn't work.

Hansen and his companion's conversation was as shrouded in mystery as the great secrets of the gay universe: why some of us have looks and others brains and why the ones with *both* are always at some *other* bar.

But, as it turned out, the attractive interloper went away alone, and Hansen continued his drinking, both of them sadder-looking, according to Nappy.

Anyway, maybe Hansen is waiting for that boy to return. But then, my irritating logic asks, who was he looking for *before* that boy came along?

Then, just the other night, I guess it was over a week ago— time passes in inaccurate increments in bars—when, while the usual crowd was talking and screeching in buzzes and blasts, someone came in.

Oddly enough, I knew who it was before I knew who it was. So to speak.

It was that boy.

I knew it because Hansen looked up and a smile sunburst across his face that made his other smiles pallid by comparison—and that's saying something.

And there was recognition…and…something else.

Love?

Listen, it's not that crazy of an idea.

Nappy raced over to my booth, with a tray of other people's drinks tinkling and slopping, and gestured excitedly toward the boy. But it was old news to me. I'd seen Hansen's face.

And the boy's.

The question that interested me—and a dozen others by then—was, "What happens now?" Were we sitting in on a brief but splendidly crucial moment in romantic history in the making?

Hansen and the boy met. Warmly.

Touched hands. Tenderly.

And they went to a booth across from mine, falling into the kind of surroundings-eliminating conversation only possible between intimates. Or would-be intimates. Some light-voiced laughs but mostly quiet, genteel talk. Warm tones. Lovers' tones.

The boy was beautiful. His eyes sparkled in the booth's candlelight. (Maybe *that's* the kind of writing that keeps me where I am, but, damn it, it was true!)

He was the Boy Next Door, the Fairy-tale Prince (in any fairy tale). And for *my* money, he was in love like crazy with Hansen. But who among us wasn't?

Even if only for a minute or two.

Hansen looked calm, but he was flushed, and his eyes had an unusual glint. There was something in them reserved for other than ordinary mortals.

The regulars were buzzing. All the dyed-in-the-hair, cynical, know-the-ropes barflies bonded briefly, like aging Southern belles hiding behind frilly fans to comment on the unfolding occasion.

A storybook romance had echoed through our odd little establishment's accumulation of myths and anecdotes for something like two years...and there we all were, on the edges of our well-worn seats. Without watching, everybody watched Hansen and the beautiful, shy young man.

Without caring, everybody cared.

Hansen moved closer, eyes deepening to drink in more of the unheard words that, judging from the young boy's expression, had to be about love.

Older pairs of eyes met—weary, bleary, all kinds. We were wondering: *If we silently held our breaths and thought good thoughts, would we be able to add at least this one happy ending to the arsenal of failed fairy tales?*

About half an hour before closing time—I'd hung around expressly to "observe"—Hansen and the boy began conversing at lengthening intervals. But their expressions told enough.

The boy appeared content.

He looked only at Hansen. Saw only him.

And Hansen looked...

...slowly...

...at the door.

I stopped drinking mid sip.

Hansen's eyes rested—fleetingly—on the door of the bar.

The boy's eyes followed Hansen's gaze. Followed his line of sight to the door.

Hansen looked back at the boy, and then, as if caught doing something embarrassing, his eyes darted down to the tabletop.

The boy got up. And left some money next to his glass.

Hansen stared up at him, questioningly.

The boy smiled sadly, faintly, and—am I *crazy?*—pityingly at Hansen.

And turned away.

The boy made his way down the aisle and out that door at which Hansen had looked and had *been* looking—for how long now? For what? For whom?

And then the boy was gone.

Gone, I knew—we *all* knew—for good.

Hansen's been back every night since then, of course. He still gets a lot of attention, mostly from the newer faces. Not so much from us regulars. He still talks a lot. Dances a little. Leaves alone. He still looks at the door regularly, over the shoulder of whomever he's sitting with.

But you know, I've decided it's time for me to move on. I've decided that I'm not going to wait around to find out who Hansen is waiting for.

I don't even think Hansen knows.

My First Pickup Line
by Ethan Brandon

It was a dump, but it had a dance floor. And that made it beautiful to me.

My first night in Atlanta. The night before my first day of my first job in Atlanta. And my first visit to a gay bar.

Oh, it wasn't my first night "out." That had been some six months earlier, in Knoxville, Tennessee, July 4th, in fact. Independence Day, though that bit of irony didn't hit me until the next afternoon as I reflected on the night before, a night that had begun on a neighbor boy's front porch and ended on the floor of my apartment. In the days and weeks that followed my sexual declaration of independence, I'd become a part of the Knoxville gay subculture, and, as "fresh meat," I'd had my share of sexual opportunities. But it was always at someone's party, someone's apartment, for "K-town" had only two gay bars, tiny places located down back alleys I wouldn't have visited in broad daylight, much less at night. Plus I had the fresh-out-of-the-closet fear that every new gay boy has about entering his first gay bar. So I stuck to private parties.

But now I was in Atlanta, having landed a radio job in suburban Marietta that would start the next morning. I'd arrived that afternoon, found a motel for me, my Camaro-full of belongings, and my cat. And now, armed with a map of a city I'd explored for a month while job hunting, I headed in search of a bar I'd heard about from Knoxville friends.

The Joy Lounge was a two-story house, the first floor of which had been converted to a bar. It faced Ponce DeLeon, a main east-west drag north of downtown Atlanta, with an adjacent gravel parking lot. I probably noticed it was gravel that first night, but it didn't become important until a few months later when, while escaping through the back door from a police raid, I fell and cut my hands on the stones—a fact I was unaware of until arriving safely home and noticing blood on the steering wheel. But that's another bar story.

It was a Monday night, and the front room of tables was empty. A few dozen people occupied the back room, a room consisting of the bar, a few booths and tables, and—oh, yes— a dance floor. Well, at least a space from which tables had been removed and where a jukebox had been placed. Yes, a jukebox. This was just six months after Stonewall, and gay club life hadn't yet entered the disco era of lighted dance floors and DJ booths. In fact, the police raid I mentioned was because the club wasn't supposed to have a dance floor, at least not one on which boys danced with other boys.

My presence immediately drew attention. I was short (very short), blond (bleached blond), young (24 and looking 16, if that), and not exactly (well, not at all) a stud. But I *was* fresh meat. The scent of freshly-packed USDA prime gay boy was instantly picked up on.

I'd been accustomed to this at some Knoxville parties, but there I had friends to protect me. This night I was on my own. So I headed for the bar and ordered a beer. I perched on a stool from which my very short legs dangled and turned my face to the bar.

My defensive technique worked too well. While eyes were still upon me, no one approached or spoke. Finally, I turned to the boy on the next stool and started to speak, only to realize I had no idea what to say. "Come here often?" seemed too trite. "God, you're incredibly cute!" seemed too forward. Until now I'd never had to come up with an opening line. Others had offered theirs to me.

So I did the obvious. I briefly stared, then looked away, then stared again, then looked away. Smooth operator I was. Real smooth.

Then someone played the jukebox, a great dance number. I was definitely a dancing fool, if not yet a dancing queen. So I turned again and asked the cute boy, "Wanna dance?" That I'd never danced with another boy—much less asked one to dance—didn't matter. Another first for a first night.

"All right," came his plaintive reply, and we headed for the dance floor where we stayed for, oh, maybe three songs. They were all fast, so we never touched, but then came a slow song, and in another first night first, I was dancing in the arms of another boy, a boy named Danny.

From the time of my first-grade dancing-school lessons, I'd loved to dance—even if I'd never learned to love girls. And the girls I'd never learned to love loved to dance with me. My above-average dancing ability was a saving social grace for a guy not otherwise likely to be a "chick magnet." I knew how to hold a girl; I knew how to lead. And I guess the girls might have liked the way my hands never wandered when I held them, although they may not have known *why* they didn't wander.

But dancing with Danny was different. It was almost like coming out all over again. If I'd had any doubts about who I was after that personal Independence Day, those doubts faded in Danny's arms. Yep, I was gay all right. I was a boy who was born to dance with other boys. I was in an unfamiliar town, in an unfamiliar place, with an unfamiliar boy, but it all seemed so familiar. The anxiety I should have felt was absent. The Joy Lounge might as well have been called Heaven, for that's certainly where I was. It was a tiny, dumpy, hole-in-the-wall, police-protection–paying Heaven, but that didn't matter. I was there, and so was Danny, and we were slow dancing.

The music ended, for it was closing time, just before midnight. Yep, midnight, the hour when beer-only bars had to close. Danny and I returned to our bar stools to finish our beers and make our respective exits.

"So, what are you going to do now?" Danny asked.

It was time for a final first.

"I'm taking you home with me," I replied.

"You are?"

"Of course I am. You're going home with me."

And he did. The next day I moved in with him.

My first pickup line. And it worked.

Bless You, Bella
by Duc DeForge

We were an eclectic bunch. Our energetic and self-appointed leader was Bella, a 50-ish hairdresser who worked at a salon for elderly but elegant dowagers. When not rinsing blue hair bluer or attempting to tease 16 strands of black-dyed hair into a whole hairdo, Bella was on the go. There wasn't a bar in D.C. that didn't welcome him with open arms—and with good reason. He made a lot of money, and he absolutely loved to spend it—in bars. Other than working, passing out for a few hours rest each night, and masturbating, Bella's time was spent in a bar, drinking. And Bella did not nurse a drink or drink sissy drinks. Martinis, manhattans, and Rob Roys were de rigeur for cocktail hour. After that it was time for serious drinking: vodka or scotch, depending on mood.

Not that Bella was *always* in a bar, just usually. There was the occasional party, the occasional dinner out. But stops at bars before and after such events were likely. Even a trip to Florida, Rehoboth Beach, or Philadelphia meant drinks along the way and a stop at a local gay bar the minute you arrived, no matter what the hour.

Groups hung around Bella like...like young unwealthy homosexuals to a hard-drinking, free-spending hairdresser. But that wasn't his only attraction. Bella was entertaining beyond belief—full of jokes, informed, and eager to discuss any topic. Plus he'd been around forever. He had arrived in D.C. 35 years earlier and never left. He knew everyone and everything. His repertoire of stories could never be exhausted; each anecdote reminded him of six more. The fun never stopped—until Bella would have that fatal drink and turn vicious and obnoxious. But that's another story.

Gregarious and fond of the spotlight, Bella held court wherever he chose. He never traveled alone, so if a bar had just opened or was still relatively quiet, his arrival signaled party time. The best part was that everyone was welcome—old, young, fat, skinny, black, white, man, woman, or anything in between.

That's where I come in.

I had gone through a messy divorce and spent two years working two jobs to pay off the expenses. To celebrate paying them off, my parents had invited me to spend a week with them in Rhode Island at Naragansett Beach. One night I went off on my own and ended up at a summer-stock performance. During intermission I chatted with some "theatrical" types and was invited to a cast party after the show. I went and had a great time. By the time I paused for a quick nap about eight hours later, I had been in almost all of the six bedrooms, with a different combination of men and women in each. I never met a combination I didn't like! As I drove away that afternoon, one of my male playmates said, "I'm from D.C. too. Hope I run into you at the Georgetowne Grille."

One Saturday night a few weeks after my return to Washington, guess where I felt like going? Only thing was, I couldn't remember the name of the place. I drove to Georgetown anyway. Too embarrassed to ask the whereabouts of a homosexual hangout, I decided to pick out queer-looking guys and follow them. This was distressing; I would hear two guys discussing decorating or recipes and fall in behind them, only to end up at some ultramixed club celebrating some girl's engagement or birthday. Three hours later, with no possibility of lurid sex in sight, I headed back to my car. Right in front of my spot was an unmarked door leaking good, loud music. I thought, *What the hell, have a drink and head back to the burbs.*

I walked in and found my den of iniquity.

In a not-too-large square room were small tables cramped together, with men sitting shoulder to shoulder around them. In the dense cloud of smoke floating above the patrons, I made out the figure of a well-tanned blond man walking on top of the tables, dodging drinks and ashtrays, from one end of the room to the other. When he reached his destination and climbed back to earth, a cheer rang out, "Hurrah, Bella's not drunk yet!" I stood at the bar for the longest time—almost two cigarettes worth—waiting for service, until the only waitress in the place confided loudly, "Hey, cutie, better sit down if you want a drink. You're in D.C. No seat, no service!"

That's when Bella careened across the room, grabbed my hand, and pulled me back to his table. When I saw no empty chairs, I asked where I should sit. "On my face, gorgeous, on my face!" At which point hoots and whistles flourished.

Thus began my ten-year odyssey in Bella's land of bars.

Washington's blue laws were abolished during this period, allowing customers to stand. As a result, a new type of gay bar emerged. Within months three new bars opened in rapid succession on the same block. One was a late-night disco. Another was part disco, part upscale lounge and restaurant. The third was Mr. P's.

Mr. P's first floor contained a large bar with a pool table and, in an adjacent room, a dance floor. The second floor housed another bar, with videos, a blacked-out hallway, and an outdoor terrace. The place became a hangout for all types: Levi-leather types lounged around the second floor, watching porno and groping each other and anyone else who strayed in; sunbathers nursed frozen cocktails on the patio; disco queens whirled around the tiny dance floor; and we hard-core boozers crowded the main bar and pool-table area. Disco Granny, an 80-something fag hag, would come roller-skating in on Saturday afternoons. Wall-to-wall mirrors brought cruisers on Saturday nights. On Sunday nights Mr. P's overflowed with drag queens on their night off. Weekday happy hour here was the best in town—free hors d'oeuvres abounded. The bartenders were hunky and friendly; free, heavy-handed drinks from them and the owners were frequent. So we practically lived there.

Mr. P's recognized the importance of Bella types and catered to making him and his crowd feel at home. Stools were reserved; bar tabs could be paid weekly; poor conduct was overlooked; IDs were not checked. We were bar gods!

Mr. P's was the first to start celebrating holidays in a big way, celebrating any kind of event for days before and after the actual date. The first sign of spring brought the annual Patio Opening Party. Beach balls, frozen drinks, and umbrella tables were scattered around for a week before and after. The climax was a drag bathing-beauty contest. Naturally, Mardi Gras was special, and even Cinco de Mayo. Most of the occasions prompted some kind of costume contest, and Mr. P's encouraged participation by giving out large cash prizes to the winners. None of our crowd entered the contests, but Bella insisted we mark the occasions somehow—maybe a mask, a cape, or just a scarf to declare us participants and not just onlookers.

My favorite event was Halloween. One year's party stands out for me. The holiday fell on a Sunday that year, and Mr. P's hosted a big bash. Bella notified the group around noon that we should come up with costumes and meet at the bar at 7 P.M.

The night before, I had been to a house party as a hula dancer—grass skirt, lei, and a very long wig. I'd gotten trashed, though, and so had the costume. None of it was reusable. I cut the wig to shoulder length, put it on, and looked in the mirror. I had a full beard and mustache and—voila! Jesus Christ.

Instantly my costume was easy. I took an old white sheet and cut a big hole in the middle for my head. A pair of leather sandals and some twigs and clear tape fashioned into a crown of thorns completed my ensemble. I decided to be adventurous and wore nothing else underneath my makeshift robe except Jockey shorts, which I stuffed with cigarettes, lighter, money, and house keys.

The evening was lots of fun. People kept sending me drinks, the most popular being a Rusty Nail. I was asked numerous questions: "Was Peter St. Peter's real name or my nickname for him?" "Could I reverse a circumcision?" "Was Mary Magdalen a drag queen?" Many people insisted on kneeling at my feet. Several billowed under the sheet for my cigarettes whenever I wanted one. A burly leather number dragged me to the bathroom and had me piss on him while begging my forgiveness.

Along toward closing time, lust struck. Hard. A handsome, semiclad gladiator entered the room, bronze helmet encircling a pouty face and dark-blue eyes, fabulous bare chest covered in blonde fur, short suede skirt revealing muscular hairy legs twined with leather straps from knee to sandal. The crowd parted around him as he made his way directly to me. He stopped just as our faces were about to touch, scissored his arms across his chest, dropped to one knee, gazed up at me, and said,

"Lord, I am your servant."

Mesmerized, smitten, empowered, I reached down to his face and lifted it up to meet mine. The taste of many cocktails and cigarettes mingled while we kissed each other to the applause and hoots of our fellow revelers. The din only fevered our high, and oral exploration was rapidly augmented by other tactile diversions. His heavy skirt began to bulge in front and my skivvies released my stash of supplies as the elastic was stretched by hardening flesh. We agreed to leave.

His apartment was across the street, so there was no question as to our destination. Passion continued in the entry way, the elevator, and the hallway, erupting into flagrant sex the second his apartment door was opened. The first session ended, and we were still partially clothed. A quick drink and a joint rekindled the fires, but for this session costumes were abandoned, and the bed was used.

At some unrelenting hour an alarm clock beat into our heads. My Roman hero silenced it and snuggled up to me. After licking my ear for a few minutes, he hoarsely whispered, "Unless you really are who we think you are, you had best come up with a smart business suit because it's 9 o'clock Monday morning."

In minutes he was dressed and ready to leave. I, on the other hand, had problems. Since we didn't even know each other's names, he was reluctant to give me any of his clothes. And when we searched our costumes and his hiding places, we came up with exactly one dollar bill. Late, hungover, and exhausted, I redonned my costume, took the dollar, and headed for the bus stop.

The cold November wind blew my sheet in all directions, leaving me, for all intents and purposes, naked. With my wig gnarled, crown falling apart, and sheet stained with spilled drinks, dirt, and dried semen, I'm quite sure I did not resemble a risen Christ. Passersby and motorists gawked as I shivered on the corner. Fortunately I had cigarettes left.

Finally my bus arrived. All conversation and noise ceased as I climbed on and put my dollar into the fare machine. As I started down the aisle, faces stared blankly up at me. With nothing to lose I walked resolutely between the passengers, making huge signs of the cross, repeating, "Bless you, my children. Bless you."

Halloween Drag
by Christopher Lucas

"I sell refrigerators," the man said, saddling onto the stool and staring at my rouged face. There was a long pause as I said nothing. Finally I raised my thick eyebrows slightly in mock interest. "I used to go to your college," he said, as if bringing an old friend up to date. "I started working at a refrigerator repair place part-time to pay for books. You know how it is. One thing led to another, and now I sell them. I do pretty well. I hope to go into repair again and open my own shop. I never did graduate." He looked beyond me toward the pool table, waiting for me to say something, anything. Then he looked back at me, his gaze on my breasts for an impolite moment, as if *they* might talk to him since I wasn't.

I played it up just a little, twirling my stiff hair-sprayed hair behind my ear and looking bashful. I felt silly and uncomfortable wearing a dress, but it was Halloween, and I was getting drunk. I scanned the room and found Stephens playing pool. He was dressed in the only drag he knew: his fraternity colors, haphazard yellow Greek letters stitched onto a purple jersey, with the same yellow lettering painted on his cheeks. He looked like Anthony Perkins after finding his mother's makeup kit. Psychically I begged him to come and rescue me.

"I hope you don't mind me saying this, but I love your lips," the refrigerator salesman said. He stared admiringly at my Fiery Fuchsia–coated lips. "They're so full and…I don't know, warm-looking. Lips do it for me. Sure, the rest of a person is important, but God! You have beautiful lips."

I blushed—maybe because of the absurd situation or maybe because he was enamored with a part of my body I had never considered.

"My name's Ralph," he said. "May I buy you a drink?" He jiggled my almost empty vodka-cranberry, affirming I was in need of a refill. "Bartender, we'll take another one over here!" he yelled above the din of the drunk and mostly costumed revelers.

I realized he thought I was a woman. Stephens would enjoy hearing about this. "Oh, it looks like I'm next at pool. Excuse me," I said. I stood and quickly made my way to the table where Stephens was finishing a game.

"Having fun, gorgeous?" Stephens laughed, playfully pinching my ass.

"You won't believe what—" And then I felt a tapping on my shoulder. Ralph. With my new drink in hand. He smiled, held out the drink, and, noticing my pressed-on azure nails, carefully placed the vodka-cranberry in my palm. I grew flushed, embarrassed again.

"Can I play you, or are you playing with your boyfriend?" Ralph asked politely, glancing at Stephens. Stephens sized up my predicament immediately. He had a way of figuring out situations with little or no information, an ability that unnerved me.

Stephens, smiling and broadcasting machismo like an intrepid baboon, sauntered over to Ralph. I figured he was going to act like we were a couple, a charade we talked about at the beginning of the night, and that he was jealous—maybe even pretend to pick a fight with poor Ralph. "She doesn't have a boyfriend," he said into Ralph's face. Ralph, tall with broad shoulders, someone who moved refrigerators for a living, loomed over Stephens. Stephens stepped back as if he hadn't noticed Ralph's dimensions until they stood together. But Ralph's body language and positioning were not threatening; he carried himself gently. "Grab a partner, and we'll play doubles," Stephens said. To me, he giggled and punched my shoulder conspiratorially.

A few minutes later Ralph introduced us to Ivy Mandelbaum. She was dressed as a ditzy blond airline stewardess but would have looked ditzy wearing anything or nothing. She giggled when she shook hands with Stephens. When she shook my hand, her eyes descended into a sharp disapproving glare and her lips pursed. She frowned at me and grimaced through furrowed, manicured brows and then walked back to Stephens, grabbing his hand and swinging it in hers. Apparently she thought I was her competition for Stephens's affection. Apparently she also thought I was really a woman.

As we played pool, I watched Ralph. He had a charming way about him. Everything amused him, from the sour, surreptitious glares Ivy threw me to the tomboyish way I hoisted up my skirt to get a better shooting angle. His eyes glimmered when he looked at me, like he knew things I didn't and would be happy to tell me about them. I found myself smiling back and staring after him as he walked around the table. He lined up the cue ball, and when he accidentally sank it in a pocket, he raised his developed, hairy arms like two football goal posts and cheered. Ivy cheered along with him, as if she knew what was going on.

Stephens, playing his part fully, pretended to whisper sweet nothings in my ear. He said things like, "If you flip that Ivy blond over, what do you get?" Short pause. "A brunet with bad breath!" With that he'd slap my polyester-skirted ass and watch for Ivy's jealous reaction. Stephens excelled at beguiling dim-witted women.

When the game ended and we won, Ivy and Stephens sat down together. I stood near them, strategically close so I looked included in their dialogue but distant enough so Stephens could work his puerile black magic on her and score. Ralph disappeared, so when I felt safe I sat back at the bar. But before I had the chance to flag down the bartender, I felt a heavy arm around my shoulder.

"Those bathrooms can be so crowded," Ralph said to explain his absence. He sat next to me. "I hope you didn't mind I picked that Ivy as a pool partner. She was the only one I could find. She's not even close to my type." He cracked a compelling smile as he stared into my blue-lidded eyes. I gazed back, feeling warm and comfortable. For a moment I forgot I was dressed as a woman. His hand tightened around my shoulder pad and he began stroking my arm.

"Oh, my God!" I pulled away and stood up. "I gotta go!" I beelined toward the bathroom—the men's room. I pulled down my blouse and yanked out the cotton breasts held at bay by the bra, throwing them behind me. They landed in a puddle by the urinal. Struggling vainly with the clasp, I finally had to rip the straps from my shoulder to free myself from the bra. Other costumed celebrants watched my frantic spectacle and gave me wide berth. In front of the mirror, I saw the rouged face and prominent red lips stare back at me, and I felt sick. With enough rubbing, the Fiery Fuchsia came off, but my lips were still stained an unnatural crimson. A wet paper towel did nothing but streak and smear the colorings on my cheeks and eye lids. My cheeks became naturally rosy anyway as I scraped off foundation and base and scrubbed with soap and water. The sink was covered in shades of red, blue, black—the aftermath of the brutal murder of a circus clown.

I was captivated, entranced by Ralph—another man. He was handsome, with an expressive face. And I loved the way he smiled and meant it, as if for him, life was an entirely pleasant experience. I liked his shyness but also how bold he could be—complimenting my lips one moment, standing tall in front of Stephens the next. What terrified me was that he didn't know who or even what I really was.

I was attracted to men and had acted on those feelings—secretly. The fact that I could and had to love a man didn't bother me, but I wasn't ready to tell anyone yet. That would be my next, slow step in life, one I'd been planning for some time. Sometimes, though, I wondered if Stephens already knew. He understood much more than his jock party-animal persona indicated.

"Hey, beautiful," Stephens said from the rest room door. "What happened? You look like you just got mauled by a Maybelline representative."

"Ralph must think I'm really a woman. He keeps hitting on me. When he realizes I'm not, he's gonna be really pissed." What I didn't say was that I was frustrated that I found myself attracted to a man who was attracted to me as a woman. I felt like crying but held back.

"Come with me," Stephens said. "I'll take care of this." He grabbed my hand and led me to the bar.

"Ralph," he said, "I need to tell you something. My beautiful friend here is really a guy. He's my buddy. He dressed up like this," Stephens waved his hand toward me as if presenting a new contestant, "because it's Halloween. Look around you; everyone is dressed up!" Stephens seemed annoyed that he had to spell it out, like he was talking to the first-grade class he would be teaching after graduation.

Ralph looked shocked. His eyes widened, and his mouth hung open. He glanced quickly at me and then scanned the bar, as if seeing it for the first time. Football players in uniform hit on brightly clothed cheerleaders. Ghosts and guillotined kings mingled with princesses and ballerinas. Ralph's face flushed.

"Couldn't you tell by his voice that he was a guy?" Stephens asked incredulously. To me, "You kept your same voice, didn't you? I mean, you didn't pretend to be higher-pitched, right?"

"No," I said, "I didn't change my voice. I just didn't say much."

"How could you not know?" Stephens demanded. "It's Halloween!"

Ralph let out an embarrassed smile. "God! I'm so sorry," he said, turning to me. "I guess I wasn't thinking. Of course it's Halloween! I was even going to put on my work uniform and come out as myself." He laughed deeply and smiled again, his cheeks the color of Daring Damask. "I feel like such an idiot! You must think I'm some dumb hick," he said to both of us. Then he added, "I have been drinking, and I guess I wasn't paying attention. What a fool I am!"

"Well, you two work it out," Stephens said, satisfied. Smiling to me he said, "I'm going to book a flight with the stewardess over there." The dry yellow Greek lettering on his cheeks cracked and flaked. Ralph gave a sheepish smile and motioned for me to sit next to him.

"You know, I didn't get your name," he said.

"Chris, um, Christopher, actually." We reached out like men do, and I gripped his hand tightly.

"Well, Christopher, I truly am sorry. May I buy you a drink to make up for this silly evening?" He ordered a vodka-cranberry for me. "I hope I didn't make you feel uncomfortable,"

Ralph continued. "That's the last thing I'd ever do. You seem like a decent guy."

"Thank you," I said. "I've never done anything like this before. It was probably a mistake dressing up—for a few reasons." I felt I could almost tell Ralph about myself.

"Oh, I don't know," he said, regarding the ceiling, searching for words. "Sometimes we do the right things but for the wrong reasons. I don't think you made a mistake dressing like that." Ralph looked expectantly toward me like it was my turn to open up to him, then he changed the subject. "You and your friend seem quite different, but it's obvious he cares for you."

"Yeah, he's a good guy. He's a little testosterone-heavy, but he's got a good heart."

Just then Stephens and Ivy, hand in hand, walked toward us on their way to the door. Ivy looked surprised and disgusted when she saw the new breastless, makeup smeared me. "Hey," Stephens said as they passed, "I'll see you whenever. We're going back to the apartment." Then he smirked mischievously and said, "I think I saw someone kicking one of your breasts out the door of the men's bathroom. Hope you weren't planning to return it." When he passed Ralph he winked at me and raised his eyebrows, nodding his head like he approved.

Ralph and I watched them leave. When our drinks arrived and Ralph paid the bartender, I found myself staring at his serenely handsome face.

"I meant what I told you before," he said, sliding the new beverage in front of me.

"What?"

He stared for a long time, absorbing my face like a sculptor might a piece of granite. "You have beautiful lips. I meant it." Short pause. "They're so...inviting."

My polyester rump almost slid off the bar stool. I waited for the joke, but Ralph's expression did not change. "Did you know?" I asked, the words dying in my throat.

Ralph placed his large hand on my nylon knee below the bar and squeezed.

I glanced around to see if anyone noticed his hand on my leg. The Halloween partiers were oblivious. I realized that Ralph and I could be making out wildly, and we'd still be invisible to the drunken crowd.

I sat forward, close enough to feel his heat. I hadn't noticed the dimples that graced his cheeks when he was amused. They made him look playful. I smiled and sipped my drink.

No Choices (Keine Auswahl)
by Owen Levy

There was something that struck me about the guy the moment I walked through the door of Tom's Bar, Berlin's cruisiest watering hole. I spotted him leaning against the brick wall by the cigarette machine. Maybe it was the way his white headband reflected in the black light that grabbed my attention. I didn't give him a second thought, though, as I sailed through the room checking out the rest of the assembled talent.

It turned out to be the usual still life of mostly lean, leather- and denim-clad bodies posed against counters, straddling stools, or supporting assorted walls, columns, and doorjambs. Pretty crowded for a midweek evening, I thought. Showing on the big-screen monitor was an obscenely seductive video of a taut, tanned stud-puppy eagerly impaling himself on the gigantic appendage of his equally toned partner.

The taped action was momentarily diverting, and like others around me, I was captivated by the sheer pleasure reflected in the faces of the two performers. Of course, this made me horny, and I began to look closer at potential candidates.

I wandered into the john. There he was, the guy I'd noticed by the cigarette machine with the headband. In the stark fluorescent light, he was more attractive, though not necessarily my first choice. I went over and talked to him anyway because he looked like he needed to be talked to.

"*Wie geht's?*" I opened. How are you?

He shrugged.

"*Gefällt's dir hier?*" Having a good time?

"*Nein. Keine Auswahl,*" he complained. "*Überhaupt keine Auswahl!*" No, there are no choices. Absolutely nothing.

"If it were too crowded," I pointed out in my best bar Deutsch, "it would be even harder to make contact."

He said he preferred the crowded weekend nights. "On the weekends people are ready to play," he assured. "Weeknights they're more in the mood to stand around and drink, waiting until the last moment before thinking about getting off." This was his free night, and he was ready now.

He was looking better all the time. I offered to buy him a drink. He politely turned me down.

We talked further. He told me he didn't go out much, that he was in a relationship. In fact, they were both dancers with a traveling revue based in East Berlin. In winter they played provincial town halls and local theaters; in summer, the music festival circuit and big tents. He said he was classically trained.

There was no chemistry. I wished him luck and moved on.

Restlessly circling, pausing in one spot, then in another. I bought myself a drink to get next to somebody standing at the bar. No bite.

I wandered into the playroom and ran into the dancer. Once again he'd positioned himself so his headband, matching white trousers, and sleeveless muscle shirt caught the meager light just right. He was obviously in heat and connected with the first taker. It didn't work out. He moved on, getting a little closer to where I stood. Before reaching me he had another en-counter. This one lasted longer than the first, but soon he maneuvered into the corner next to me, once again positioning himself so that the light hit him just right.

We started fooling around, but it soon became obvious that he was only using me as a decoy to attract others. And gradually guys gathered. I was uncomfortable as bait, disengaged myself and moved on. Soon the little circle around him thinned, and he changed places. Somehow we ended up physically entangled once more. Though receptive, he failed to arouse me.

Coming up for air, I took a turn through the bar. Suddenly I heard my name called. A tall strawberry-blond rushed to embrace me. As he bubbled on about how glad he was to see me again in Berlin—"When did you get back? Where are you living?"—I tried to figure out who he was.

Finally he made a reference to our first meeting in New York, and I placed him. He was one of the countless fledglings a Berlin acquaintance is always giving my phone number to on their maiden voyage to America. Yes, I remembered him. His name was Holger, and we'd had lunch in a vegetarian café in midtown. Hold the sprouts, sesame-seed dressing on the side, please.

While we reminisced about our first meeting, another American I'd seen around on and off for years started playing footsie with Holger. He joined our conversation, and we were formally introduced. As we chatted the names of other mutual acquaintances popped up. It turned out we knew a lot of the same people, though he'd been in Berlin a couple of years longer.

Holger said he had something to smoke and suggested we all retreat to the dimly lit screening room and do a joint. Once we got back there, he couldn't find the piece of hash. He opined that he probably lost it at one of several earlier stops he'd made that evening. He called to an acquaintance sitting nearby and asked if he had anything. He shrugged and said he was fresh out. This fellow was yet another American. He joined us, and we arranged ourselves along the platform beneath the video screen and got acquainted. Soon there were others, and finally somebody I'd known intimately the summer before. He had something to smoke.

Our group formed an arresting tableau, backlit by the bottom quarter of the porno video: three Americans of color, lounging on a daislike platform, sex-patriots perhaps, encircled by German admirers. A smoldering offering was passed around, and with so many eager participants it was swiftly consumed. But there was enough of a buzz to achieve the desired effect, raising the frivolity quotient a notch or two.

To those who noticed us, it must have appeared that some strange drama was being played out in the whitish glow of the video. Our little spontaneous gathering was noisily laughing and joking, often shouting to be heard over the taped house music. The other patrons seemed more fascinated than annoyed, watching the screen or watching us—sometimes both.

Soon another African-American came over and introduced himself. He was in town with a touring musical and was surprised to see so many brothers gathered so far from home. The locals must have thought some sort of invasion was in progress.

Then our little brood dispersed. One said he was bored and excused himself to get a drink. Another knew of a party in Mitte, the latest trendy neighborhood. He said he was going to check it out and asked who wanted to tag along. I declined, thinking I might be better off staying put.

A rosy-cheeked brunet in sweatpants caught my eye. He was intently watching the video and, I thought, smiling at me from time to time. He seemed entertained by the action in the explicit film. I racked my brain trying to put together a witty phrase in German that might win his instant attention.

As I moved closer and got a better look, I noticed his broad, beefy hands—always a turn on for me. *Yes,* I thought, *he's the one.* When a scene on-screen of a man using a pumping device to enlarge his manhood elicited a comment from him that I didn't understand, I asked him what he had said.

He confessed he was fascinated by the pump: *"Und hab' noch nie jemand sie genutzen sehen."* He had never seen one used before.

"Ich hab' eine zu Hause!" I joked. I've got one at home.

We shared a good laugh. I should have realized I was way ahead of the game and shut up. Instead I distracted him with progressively dumb bar questions. His replies grew terser and tenser. But when somebody standing on the other side offered him a cigarette and he turned it down, I grew more determined. So few in Berlin are nonsmokers.

He moved to a nearby bench. I sat next to him and made one more attempt to engage him. Suddenly he stood, smiled, and nodded, then wandered off. I panicked. Had I blown it? When he came back he was munching the free popcorn from the bar. He didn't rejoin me on the bench but leaned against an adjacent wall. I knew it was a bad sign, but bent on making progress, I got up and circuitously ended up standing next to him.

I offered to buy him a drink.

He declined, making it clear with the look he threw me that he didn't want to be bothered any more. I moved on.

The crowd was thinning, which meant it was getting late. I wandered around anyway.

A thin blond, girlishly pretty, caught my eye. The pal he was talking to wasn't bad either. When I saw the two of them disappear into the playroom, I followed.

At first I lost them in the ebb and flow of bodies moving through the dimly lit passages but then caught sight of the blond as he took up a position in exactly the same spot where the headband-wearing dancer had stood earlier. Before I could even get close, several men moved in from various sides, and soon he was pressed against the wall in a heated embrace with one of them.

I retreated, damning myself for not being fast enough. Then I recognized the dancer standing in another corner. He was still ready for action, so we resumed fondling each other.

I cooed softly in his ear, *"Keine Auswahl. Keine Auswahl!"* No choices. No choices!

Midnight in the Garden of Evil
by Joe Frank Buckner

I didn't like the alligator. And the shirt was too tight, rubbing my nipples erect as I walked in Savannah's December night air, blowing cool off the river toward the swelling beat of music. I left my jacket in the car, not wanting to watch or check it.

Just weeks before, on my 21st birthday, I'd entered Feelgood's for the first time, consumed my first alcoholic beverage, and enjoyed my first sexual experience. Since then I had made the 55-minute journey from my hometown whenever I could escape college classes and my overprotective parents.

I slipped my frozen fingers into my jeans pockets, hoping Barry, my former psychotherapist, would be there. After I'd attempted suicide earlier that fall—prompted by an Anita Bryant–induced "homosexual panic"—my parents had delivered me to Savannah's Spreading Oaks Psychiatric Hospital, praying for a cure to my depression. God had answered through Barry, lead therapist and the first openly gay man I had ever met.

Barry had made me walk into Feelgood's that first night by myself, calling it an emotional passage on which he could not accompany me. He would be there on the other side waiting, he said, having finished his set at the piano bar on River Street where he played and sang three nights a week. He quickly became my friend and protector, and it was his idea to update my Sunday school wardrobe, including the white Izod shirt tickling my nipples. When I'd complained about how tight all of my new clothes were, he told me that I needed to display and emphasize my best assets—a "hunky chest" and a "passable ass."

That first night I had gone home with Logan, a gravelly voiced, 36-year-old with dark blond hair, blue eyes, a dark tan, and the self-assured, quiet confidence of a seasoned, middle-aged lifeguard. He too became a guardian.

Logan and I met during a breakup with his long-term lover, a model who traveled a lot. They had an on-again, off-again relationship, and I'd caught him in an off-again stage. He was upfront about it, but I was still disappointed when the cycle changed to on-again shortly after our fifth date. I had, of course, fallen in love with him. He'd been the perfect first, with his masculine, affectionate lovemaking. When he went back with his lover, he told me that although his bed was no longer available, his friendship and shoulder would always be mine.

Earlier this particular night Logan had told me he would not be going out, waiting instead for a phone call from his newly reunited lover. And I had not been able to reach Barry. This would be my first trip to Feelgood's without at least one of my guardians present.

I had been seeing a man named Will, who was to meet me later, after he had been to a formal Christmas party he committed to long before we met. Will was charming and sophisticated. He lived in an historic home filled with English antiques. I was young, country, and way out of my league with him. But his 40-year-old ice-blue eyes, soothing voice, and total attentiveness seduced me. I was in love again.

Logan winced when I told him I was seeing Will, who lived just a block away from him in the historic district. Logan called Will "the Duchess." His tone suggested it wasn't a term of endearment.

As I neared Feelgood's, I looked around to make sure no one was watching and then pressed my nipples in, trying to soften them so I wouldn't walk in feeling as if I were wearing a stripper's titty tassels. The door swung open, and a group of middle-aged drunks fell onto the street laughing and yahooing. The smell of beer, cigarette smoke, cologne, dance sweat, and poppers filled my nostrils. My groin tightened. One of the guys said, "Hiya, cutie. How'd you like to sit on my face?" He puckered his lips, air kissing as another guy pulled him across the street.

I headed directly for the bar and ordered white wine on ice. Holding the drink to my chest, I wove through the crowd to the stool by the fireplace, opposite the bar, where I felt most comfortable.

By the time I was crunching the last ice cube left in my glass, I was relaxed enough to scan the place for Barry. A mustached blond guy, 30-ish, leaning against the end of the bar nearest the dance floor, stared at me. When I could no longer avoid eye contact, he smiled and walked over.

"Hello," he said, extending his hand, "I'm Roger."

"Joe Frank."

He sipped from the drink in his left hand, and I saw a wide, gold wedding band. "Excuse me, Roger, are you married?"

He placed his palm against the wall behind me and leaned closer. "What if I am? Does that make a difference?" He nodded at my empty glass, not waiting for an answer. "What are you drinking?"

"White wine on ice, but I—" He was gone, contorting his

tall, husky frame through the maze of bodies to the bar.

I sighed and looked around, praying to see Barry, Will, or Logan, somebody to explain this married guy hitting on me. I came from a world and possessed a mind where everything was pretty much cut and dry, simple and traditional. You fell in love, married, and lived faithfully together for life. Everyone was either gay or straight, and the idea of a man married to a woman flirting with me in a gay disco was bizarre. Too bizarre.

"Thank you," I said when he brought me the drink, remembering too late Logan's admonishment not to let strangers buy me drinks.

"So, Joe Frank," he said, propping against the wall again and leaning into me. "What are you into?"

"Into?"

"Sex? What do you like to do?"

"Listen, Roger, let me ask you a question first. You're married, and you're in a gay disco? What about your wife?"

"She's a nurse. She goes in at 11, and I'm a free man all night."

"Does she know you're gay?"

"I'm not gay."

"You're not? Well, does she know you're bisexual?"

"Joe Frank, I'm heterosexual. I just like letting pretty little boys like you give me blow jobs."

I waited for the break in his expression, a laugh and a slap on my back to let me know he was playing on my obvious naïveté. But his poker face held. I looked into his green eyes, black pupils fully dilated, and knew he was serious.

"So, what about it?" he asked, rubbing his crotch against my thigh. "We could drive out to the boat ramp. Or do you have a place?"

"Sorry, but I'm waiting for someone."

"Yeah, ain't we all sugar britches." He rubbed his crotch, now hard, against me again. He lowered his mouth to my ear, "I'll wait. Some night I'll slip it between those pretty lips, and when I let you have my load, you won't care if I'm Jesus Christ." He returned to his spot across the room and resumed staring at me.

I tried not to change expression but sighed deeply without moving my chest, hoping no one would notice that my face had flushed bright red. The door opened behind me, and I heard Will's voice. *Thank God,* I thought.

"Joe Frank," he said, with a kiss and a hug. "Sorry I'm late."

"I'm just glad you're here. You look very handsome in your tuxedo. God, I'm so glad to see you."

"Are you all right?" he said, easing us back to the corner of fireplace. "You look unhappy. Are you upset with me?"

"No. I just had the strangest guy come on to me. Married."

"Point him out."

"The blond guy at the far end of the bar, the one in the camel-hair coat, leather elbow patches."

"Oh, yes. Attractive. I've seen him around." He caught my elbow and pulled me away. "I want you to meet a friend of mine. My best friend, actually. He's checking his coat."

Before we could move, another friend of Will's walked up and began a critique of the party they'd just left. Soon a tall, dark, tuxedoed man appeared in the cloak-room doorway. He pulled a white silk scarf from his neck and tossed it back to the attendant with a smile. He had a dark mustache and hair graying at the temples and above his ears. If he'd had a deeper cleft in his chin, he could have been Cary Grant's tired, slightly bloated twin. He sat at the far end of the bar and lit a thin cigar. I was struck by how comfortably he moved in his tuxedo and how completely he owned the space he filled.

Will led me directly to him. "Joe Frank, I'd like you to meet Jim Williams."

Jim stood, drawing deeply on his cigar.

"Jim, you remember me telling you about Joe Frank Buckner, from Statesboro."

"Yes, a pleasure to meet you Buck," he said, releasing smoke from his lips that rose in an elegant spiral before his face, as if he'd willed it. "Have a seat and tell me what it's like to be 19, gay, and living in Hooterville."

"I just turned 21," I said, easing onto the stool beside him.

"Well, you look 17, but I won't hold that against you."

He caught someone passing behind us by the arm. The boy nodded his head as Jim talked into his ear. It was then that I realized Will was no longer at my side. I spun around to see him on the other side of the room, by the fireplace, his voice and animated hands commanding the attention of the other tuxedoed men around him. Why, I wondered, had he left me with this man, this Savannah gay icon, this wealthy pretender of society, this man Will knew would intimidate the living hell out of me?

As much as I wanted to swing my legs away from the bar and go to Will's side, Jim's voice, his manner, his presence, would not permit me. Not to mention the fact that he had my left knee viced between his legs. It wasn't noticeable. Had someone walked up to us, it would not have been obvious that he was trying to seduce the boyfriend of his best friend.

"Your house is beautiful," I said to make conversation. "I love the way the wisteria cascades over the little entrance area."

"Buck, dear boy, nothing in Mercer house is...little."

He grinned and squeezed my knee. "You are precious. It's been a long time since I've met someone who could still blush.

Without the help of Elizabeth Arden, anyway."

I looked at my glass and realized I'd just finished the second tequila sunrise that Jim had insisted I try. He signaled the bartender to bring me another drink.

"No, thank you. I think I've had enough. I haven't eaten much today."

"I saw you last Saturday," he said with a wink, resting his elbow on the bar to bring his face closer to mine.

"Saturday? Where?"

"Don't you remember where you were last Saturday?"

"I was apartment-sitting for Barry."

"I know," he said.

Barry's apartment was one block closer to Jim's than Will's house, but I was still puzzled. "So where did you see me?"

"When you were cruising Forsythe."

"Cruising? I was jogging around the park."

"Whatever you say, Buck." His hand rested on the bar near mine, my fingers clutching my glass. He rubbed the back of my hand with his forefinger. "I guess there aren't any places to jog in Hooterville, so you had to travel all the way to Savannah to pump those buns."

"How did you know it was me?" I said, raising my glass to my lips.

"Will showed me a photograph."

"He did?"

"You were in his robe, sipping orange juice on the sofa in his den, or whatever he calls that damned dark-green room." His fingertips brushed lightly over my hair. "Those dark curls were still wet from your morning-after shower. And you still had the soft radiance of the freshly fucked."

My ears felt fevered, red-hot. Something was wrong, but I wasn't savvy enough to grasp what. A game was being played, but no one had told me the rules. "I wonder what happened to Will," I said, looking across the room. "He was over by the fireplace."

"Buck," he said, tapping the nub of his cigar in an ashtray. "How would you like to sip orange juice with me at Mercer House in the morning?"

"Sure, what time would you like Will and me to walk over?"

He laughed, slightly choking on a swallow of his drink. "My, but you are precious. Coy? Coquettish? I thought it was a lost art."

I felt Will's arm on my shoulder. "How are things in this corner of the house?" I relaxed when Will rubbed my neck.

"Oh, Buck and I are old friends now," Jim said. He winked at Will. "He's everything you said. Why didn't you bring him to the party tonight?" He stood, placed a hand on Will's shoulder, and whispered briefly in his ear. His eyes dropped to me: "Excuse me for a moment, please."

Will sat on the edge of Jim's stool. "Isn't he a charming rascal?"

"Will, listen. Look at me," I stammered. "Will, Jim…"

"What? Did Jim say something to you?"

"He's been trying to pick me up."

"Would that be so bad?" he said scanning the crowd. "To wake up in Mercer House?"

"What do you mean? I'm with you. Will?"

"Oh, Joe Frank, loosen up," he said, standing as if to better search the faces in the throng of bodies. "We've had our thing, and Jim is a delight. And besides, you'll like him in bed."

I felt more benumbed than ever. As I turned my knees outward, hoping to stand, Jim reappeared, moving between Will and me, resting a hand on my shoulder. Will lit another cigar for him, and Jim blew the first smoke over my head as he gently rubbed my shoulder. The ensuing silence, the smiles Will and Jim shared, their nearness to me caused my mind to reel and pitch. I wasn't sure if I was going to knock them both on their asses or if the floor would split open and the earth swallow me up.

Neither happened. Instead Logan appeared. He stepped between Jim and me, asking "You OK?"

I shook my head no.

He pulled me away, led me to the door. "Wait here for me, OK? I'll only be a minute, and then we can go home. I left a fire in the fireplace."

I watched Logan berate Will and Jim, thinking I had never known so many words to come out of his mouth at one stretch. Will finally turned away, blue eyes flashing anger or maybe fear. He slipped into the hall leading to the bathroom and cloak room. As I shivered at the doorway, Logan stared Jim down, literally, until Jim sat on the stool and turned his back.

Logan returned, his face a portrait of deep satisfaction. We stepped into the now-cold night, and Logan lay his fur-lined, black leather jacket over my shoulders.

"You said you weren't coming out tonight."

"I hadn't planned to, but I started thinking about you with Will. And I knew Barry was at his Mama's in Alma, so—"

"I am so stupid!"

"No, you're not. You're just too trusting. Barry or I should have warned you about those two broken down queens. I wanted to say something about Will when you first started seeing him, but Barry said you had to learn some things on your own. Jim Williams, that pompous shithead!"

We rode the rest of the way in silence. As we drove past Will's house, I looked at the lights and knew I'd never enter that house again. Just a couple of blocks east was Logan's car-

riage house apartment. Logan, Barry, Will, and Jim Williams
all lived within walking distance of each other. I suddenly realized how much of an outsider I was in Savannah.

I warmed my body in front of Logan's fireplace and laughter unexpectedly sputtered out of me.

"What's so funny?" Logan asked, reclining on the sofa.

"I don't know," I said. "I'm just glad I'm here. Glad you
found me tonight."

"Me too. The Duchess and the Dark Queen almost had you."

He motioned for me to come to him. I lay back against his
chest, and his arms wrapped around me. "Logan, was Will just
passing me along to Jim? Or were they trying to...to...get me
in a three-way?"

"Doesn't matter. You were going to be used, used in a way
you couldn't handle, used up and tossed to the curb. And then
they'd be looking for fresh meat again. Heartless bitches."

"What did you say to Jim?"

"Well, we just had a word of prayer."

"No, really, what did you say to him?"

"I just talked to him in a language he understands. You see,
Jim Williams is really a redneck from some town near Macon.
And right now he'd rather slap a rattlesnake than mess with ei-
ther of us."

Later, after dozing in front of the fire, we began undressing
for bed. "Leave your briefs on," Logan said. "Don't tempt me.
I'm married again."

"You want me to sleep on the sofa? I should sleep on—"

"Get your ass in bed."

He held the covers for me, and I slid to his body. My back-
side fit snugly against him, and he wrapped his arms around
me. I felt his chest hair against my back, the warmth of his
body, and felt safe. He kissed my neck and nuzzled his face in

the cradle of my neck and shoulder. "You have a sweet soul, Joe Frank. If not for Bob and if you were about ten years older…"

"Yeah, yeah, yeah," I said. "And if I only had a brain." We both laughed. "Thanks, Logan." I kissed the palm of his hand three times. "Thanks for rescuing me."

"Put those lips on me again, and one of us *will* have to sleep on the sofa." He pulled a pillow between his crotch and my ass. "Now be a good boy and go to sleep."

But I couldn't sleep. I kept replaying what had happened at Feelgood's, trying to decide what I should have done differently. And I wondered when I would stop being ignorant. And why Logan drank so much Scotch. And I thought about how much I loved Logan and how much more I could easily love him and how he would never be over Bob. And I thought about what would happen when their cycle hit off-again and Logan could remove that pillow. And then I felt guilty for thinking such a thing.

It was December of 1978. Just four years later, a short distance away, in a room at Mercer House, Jim Williams shot and killed Danny Hansford, his 21-year-old lover. And 12 years after that, John Berendt's book *Midnight in the Garden of Good and Evil* was published, and a movie was made, and Jim Williams was painted as an endearing rogue. But to me he will always be the Dark Queen.

An Amsterdam Night
by David May

The Amsterdam Eagle, like the Argos just across the notorious Warmoesstraat, was all anyone could expect: a maze of back rooms, cages, toilets, and booths filled with the smell of sex, grunting men coupling in plain sight or behind locked doors, and the occasional smack of flesh hitting flesh, followed by the ever grateful groan. Urgent whispers in half a dozen languages filled my ears, broken by the barked commands, hungry pleas, and grateful sighs I'd understand in any language.

I'd returned to Amsterdam hoping it was as wonderful as I'd remembered and afraid I might be disappointed since no reality could possibly live up to my memories of this sacred place. Anxious to relive the joy and spontaneity of sex between strangers that had disappeared in the States, I was back in the pocket of civilization I had come to think of as my second home, a city and a country invincible to the Puritan backlash that had swept North America, the United Kingdom, and much of Europe during the 1980s.

Not much of a drinker, I bought a Coke and made my way to the back of the bar and waited. It was only 11 o'clock—early for a Thursday, the first night of the weekly long weekend the city promoted to tourists from Britain and Europe who flocked there looking for the party they'd never find at home. Most wouldn't go home until Sunday evening, others not until Monday night or even Tuesday morning, all of them wanting to make the most of their short holiday.

I lit a small cigar and watched the parade of men increase in number as midnight drew nearer. They were North American, Spanish, Turkish, Scandinavian, Israeli, and who knew what else. I put out my cigar, finished my Coke, and let my dick lead me where it wanted to go, into the back of the narrow bar, into the recesses of half-lit rooms and narrow stairways where the smell and sound of man sex was thick as a San Francisco fog.

I saw him leaning against a post almost immediately. We glanced at each other, liking what we saw. Both of us were bearded, muscular men around six feet tall, though he lacked the love handles I had carried from birth. I wondered what he was in the mood for, top or bottom, and then wondered the same thing about myself. I walked deeper into the darkness, admiring what I saw, excited by what I heard, wanting to be a part of it. I made a loop back, and he was still there. We looked at each other again, the spark of mutual desire lighting the air. I approached. He nodded. We kissed.

Our tongues met, each of us exploring the other's mouth, hoping to find the deepest part of ourselves in the kiss, looking for the special magic button that would send the other over the edge. I lost myself in the kiss. Our mouths stayed locked for long minutes, separating only to catch our breath, then rejoining. He ran his hands over my body, pushed aside my leather jacket to pull on my nipples, undid my Levis to grab my butt with both hands and pull me closer.

He wore sweatpants and no underwear. I felt his magnificent cock poking upward and reached into his sweats and caressed it—large and thick, typical of Dutch men, uncut but immaculately clean, as is also their wont. I had to have it.

I knelt, swallowing as much of his tool as I could, trying hard not to choke. His hips moved back and forth, and his cock found the back of my throat. I took all that I could, felt the head of his dick in my esophagus, and backed off before I passed out.

I stood, and he pulled me to him, kissing me as he had before, swallowing me in his kiss. Each of his hands grabbed an ass cheek, pulling them apart. I let my Levis drop to my knees, pulled back his foreskin, slick with my spit, and slipped his cock between my legs. He moved between my thighs as we kissed, thrusting just beneath the hole he searched for and wanted. I felt a finger in my fuck hole. I groaned softly as his tongue moved further down my throat and his free hand pulled me closer. Then he slapped my ass—the trick to sending me over the edge. I was in heaven. I was his.

Suddenly he pulled away. "Shall we have a drink?" he asked in perfect and beautifully accented English.

I almost laughed but didn't.

"Yeah," I answered, catching my breath. "That would be great."

This was one of the amusing idiosyncrasies common to the Dutch. It didn't matter that we were on the verge of fucking; good manners called for a social exchange of some kind. We should at least know each other's names before we did it.

"What would you like?" he asked.

"*Spa Root,*" I replied, asking for the local equivalent of a Calistoga.

He looked at me a moment with a surprised smile. "You learn quickly."

"I try."

He ordered my *Spa Root* and *een pilsje* for himself.

"Dank u," I said, hoping to dazzle him with one of my few Dutch phrases.

He handed me my drink, and we clinked bottles.

"Proost!"

"I'm Huib."

"David."

"Where are you from?"

"San Francisco."

"Ah! We get a lot of men from San Francisco here."

"I'm not surprised."

He nodded. "You know a little *Nederland,* I see."

"Just enough to be polite."

"That's very sweet of you," he said, putting his free hand on my ass again and pulling me a little closer. "But unnecessary."

His mouth reached out for mine, and I was lost to the world. I felt his cock harden again through the fabric of his sweats. His hand moved to the crack of my ass, caressing the seam that formed the crevice in my jeans.

A moment later we were apart, panting, staring at each other.

"What shall we do about this?" he asked.

An odd turn of phrase, I thought. I wondered if he'd learned it from a Brit he'd picked up. It sounded like something a Brit would say. In any case, the answer seemed pretty obvious. Did he want me to draw him a picture?

I nodded back toward the backroom.

He smiled.

A moment later we were behind a locked door. I was on my knees applying the condom, lubing it, stroking it, getting it ready for my hole. When I stood Huib lubed my ass for me, stretching it open in preparation for the fat piece of meat he was about to shove inside me.

"Take it easy at first," I whispered. "I haven't had anything that big up my ass in a long time."

He smirked the self-satisfied smile of a well-hung man who has once again been assured of his exceptional size. I leaned over, my back to him, smiling to myself and knowing I'd inadvertently added the aphrodisiac of a well-stroked ego.

I felt him enter me. I winced, put my hand out, signaling him to pause. He did. Then, like the expert he clearly was, he pushed in further as he felt my fuckhole relax, moving steadily forward until all nine fucking inches were in my ass. I groaned with delight, threw my head back, and yelled out one of the first Dutch phrases I'd ever learned: *"Neuk me!"*

Huib took me at my word and went to town.

Now it was us making the noise of sex, the grunting, the groaning, the slapping. Sweet and guttural Dutch obscenities streamed from Huib's mouth like water. My sexual vocabulary, in Dutch anyway, was limited to that one single cry—repeated again and again as I pressed the wall to keep from being knocked against it. I felt as well as heard the wooden cabin creak and rock around us as I held myself steady against Huib's brilliant assault.

Huib's cock pushed, pulled, and pounded me, punishing my prostate to a level of passion I'd not felt with a stranger in years. His hand slapped my ass again and again as he grunted his pleasure, his joy, his satisfaction in my willingness to be his hole. I was the lucky boy who was the place he put his fat man-meat tonight, happy to be the one he wanted, the one he fucked and filled. I grunted and groaned my satisfaction, hoping the whole world heard us, that everyone in Amsterdam knew that tonight I was this hot man's fuckhole.

After holding off for I don't know how long, he grabbed my waist and raped my ass with renewed fury. I whacked at my cock with equal intensity, screaming for him to come, to come so hard I would taste it through the condom. Then, with one last thrust, he growled his last growl, grunted his last coarse phrase, and collapsed on top of me. I felt his cock expand and explode. I blew my own load at the same time, shooting it against the wall of our little cabin. I almost collapsed but managed to lean against the wall and support both our weights.

I heard Huib catching his breath, felt the sweat pour off his face and chest and down my back until it reached the crack of my ass. Then he regained himself, pulled himself up, and slowly removed his beautiful, uncut cock. There was an audible pop, and I felt its absence, felt it leave where I was sure it belonged.

I turned around and watched as he peeled off the condom, then held it up so I could see the little come-filled sack, the sight of which is always a part of my sexual satisfaction—an erotic image to store away and remember in the years to come. Then we kissed, long and deep for several minutes. For a moment I wished we were in my hotel room, in bed and ready to fall asleep next to each other, knowing he would be up and ready to fuck me again first thing next morning. Then I remembered myself.

He smiled. I smiled.

"Another beer?" I offered, not wanting to let go of him just yet but knowing I must since my own lover was out on Warmoesstraat somewhere, possibly looking for me at that very instant. And if Huib and I ran into him in the bar, I knew that Huib, being Dutch, would handle it all with great aplomb and courtesy, ending the evening by kissing us both good night and agreeing to meet us for dinner later in the week. He would (and did) do all of this because he was a civilized man from a civilized city in a civilized country—a man who, if circumstances had been different, I would probably have loved.

The Catalyst
by Brian Cochran

It was the bar of the summer that year, another in a long list of flash-in-the-pan successes, its fame so momentary that, many years later, I no longer remember its name. The building on Cheshire Bridge Road that housed the bar is still there, though, currently occupied by a titty bar; apparently Atlanta can never have too many.

The bar was inadequately air-conditioned, especially for a typically humid Southern summer. At closing time, 2 A.M., when the lights went on for those of us who were foolish enough or desperate enough to have stayed past last call, the floors would be filthy and wet from the runoff in the bathrooms, the toilets and urinals having leaked their contents all night. The muck from the bathrooms mixed with sweat, spilled drinks, and, more than likely, spilled semen, making the bare concrete floor slimy and perilous.

It was a Thursday, a steamy night when few queens bothered to venture out. I was out only because my lover Dan had insisted we go.

"Just for a little while," he whined. "It's almost the weekend." Most people would say that pouting never looks attractive on a broad-shouldered man who is over six feet tall, but it always worked with me.

I would have preferred to stay home, since I liked to restrict my bargoing to weekends. At the age of 25, I was already finding it difficult to go to work the next morning after a night out. Dan, older than me by five years, had no such trouble. He never seemed to suffer the ill effects I did after a night of drunkenness and went to his job as a middle manager at a local bank as cheerfully as always the next day.

Of course, being tired and cranky afterward was not the only reason for my reluctance, for I knew Dan's ulterior motive. It had only been a couple of months since he had declared our two years of monogamy over and our relationship "open." Dan was looking to get laid—and not by me. Or, more precisely, not by only me.

I fell in love with Dan when he was dating my best friend, Myra (OK, Fred). Myra had been seeing Dan for about a month, when, on a night we were all out together at the Pharr Library (another defunct bar, but at least I remember that one's name), Dan sidled up to me and suggested we get together. As in, right then.

Only someone terrifically naive could have believed this would turn out agreeably for everyone involved. Unfortunately I was plenty naive. I went to the underground parking garage with Dan, leaving Myra to wonder where we'd gone, and Dan and I had first-time, admittedly mind-blowing sex in the back seat of his Chevette. Not exactly first class, but it seemed awfully hot and glamorous at the time. As I said, I was naive.

The mind-blowing sex continued, of course. And Myra found out, of course. (Dan told her.) Myra told me where to get off, as well she should have, and Dan and I moved in together.

I once heard someone theorize that one should never move in with someone while the sex is still hot. The chemical mix ricocheting around in your brain renders you stupid. The theory is sound; I'm living proof.

While Dan may not have been a good choice for a life partner, he was great in bed. Even after two years, we were still passionate. At least *I* thought so. But Dan wanted more. He wanted to "trick out," as he so winningly put it.

So we ended up at this bar on a Thursday night. I wouldn't have gone but was too jealous to let Dan go alone. I didn't want a repeat of the previous Saturday's morning scene, when I stumbled into the kitchen and found Dan sitting at the table having his first cup of coffee with a hunky blond stranger.

"Why don't you make us some breakfast?" Dan had said, laughing callously. "How about some of your famous biscuits?"

That alone would have sent most people scurrying to the phone book to check on rental rates for moving vans, but not me. I thought it was just a phase Dan was going through, and I was determined to tough it out with him, however unhappy it made me.

It was already late when we walked into the bar, which was already steamy from the lack of circulating air. When our eyes adjusted to the darkness, we made our way toward our first drink.

It wasn't busy, and we were immediately served by a face that was familiar to me, though it was no one I had ever met personally and it wasn't his face I particularly remembered. Our bartender was the star of several porn films I had seen and was a minor local sensation because of his legendary endowment. Actually, when you met him in person, it all became a bit less impressive, as he was only about 5 feet 2 inches tall, which, proportionally speaking, made his above-average cock look huge. Since meeting him, I've noticed that it's that way with a lot of porn stars. The next time you're watching a porn movie (and I know you do) check out the guy's height as compared to, oh, say, a door frame.

The bartender's *nom de porn,* I knew, was Dick Fisk.

"What can I get for you, dolls," he asked, his bare chest about level with the bar. I will say this, he had two of my favorite things (or is it four?) going for him: beautifully sculpted pecs and round, dark nipples, even if they were in miniature.

"Oh, I don't know," Dan replied, tilting his head at an unflattering, girlish angle. "Why don't you surprise me?" Dan had the irritating habit of acting as if I were not in the room whenever he zeroed in on a potential trick. Singular pronouns were his specialty.

"How about you, hon?" the bartender asked.

"The same," I said. It makes me want to kick myself all the way to Alabama and back now, but in those days I had no guts.

The bartender winked at me and turned to his work. I glared at Dan, who was too busy mentally rimming the bartender's curvy ass to notice.

The porn-star bartender returned with a pair of shot glasses filled with something white and foamy.

"What are these?" Dan asked.

"They're called Russian Quaaludes. Try it. You'll like it," he said, and went off to serve another guy.

Dan downed his in one gulp. "Pretty good," he said, wiping a bit of foam off his lip.

"What's in it?" I asked.

"Tastes like a milk shake. Try it, sissy." Dan knew exactly which of my buttons to push. I hated being called a sissy. Leftovers from high school, I guess.

I downed mine as Dan had, in one great gulp. It really was pretty good.

Meanwhile, Dan, I noticed, had planted himself resolutely at the bartender's station. As I said, he had already staked out his prey.

In minutes the bartender was back. "What did you think?" he asked. "Like 'em?"

Dan leaned in. "Uh-huh. What else you got that tastes good?"

"You'd be surprised," the bartender said, winking and returning Dan's leer.

But I wouldn't, I thought, having already seen his surprises on video.

It wasn't that I was a prude—far from it. But the way Dan approached his conquests turned my stomach. Not that he had approached me any differently.

In minutes the bartender was back with more shooters. "On the house, babe," he said to Dan.

"Thanks," Dan said. "I'll have to think of some way to repay you." The bartender smiled noncommittally and walked away again.

I downed my second shot. *If nothing else,* I thought, *I can at least get blasted.* For free, it looked like, thanks to Dan's cheesy, maladroit banter. "Oh, well," I said, downing a third shooter, might as well take advantage of the porn-star bartender's largesse. After a while the bartender joined in, and we were all doing shots together.

About an hour later I was leaning against the bar, foraging in the bartender's garnish tray for something edible. I was hoping for olives but settled for squashed, sugary, candy-apple red cherries. Dan and the bartender seemed close to making a date, and I had had, oh, six? eight? 1,000? free shooters.

"So, what are you doing after," the bartender asked Dan.

"Depends on you." My stomach lurched.

"I like to go out after we close," the bartender said. "To unwind, you know?"

"Sounds good." Another lurch.

"Dan," I said, swallowing hard. The sparse crowd at the bar had thinned out even more. Dan and the bartender were making eyes. My stomach was doing Cirque du Soleil somersaults.

"Dan, I need to go," I choked out. "Please."

"Excuse me for a minute," Dan said to the bartender. He turned to me, his face hidden from the bartender's view. "What the hell is your problem?" he snarled.

"I'm going to be sick. I need to go home," I said, holding a hand over my mouth.

"Damn it," Dan said under his breath. "I know why you're doing this, you little shit."

He turned back to the bartender, with his happy face on again. They conferred for a minute, then Dan turned back to me.

"OK, let's get out of here," Dan said, storming out of the bar, leaving me to follow.

Outside, away from the stifling heat inside the bar, I felt a little better. But my head spun when we tried to cross Cheshire Bridge Road to get to our car. Still, I managed to cross five lanes of traffic safely, with cars full of people as drunk as I was, more than likely, considering the number of drinking establishments in the area. When I finally got to the other side of the road, I was too off-balance to walk, and sat on the curb.

"Get up. Let's go," Dan ordered, flinging open his car door. "You wanted to go home, let's go."

With supreme effort, I picked myself up and threw myself into the passenger seat. We pulled onto the road and had gone maybe a mile before I felt very, very sick again.

"Pull over," I said.

"What?" Dan said.

"Pull over. I'm going to be throw up."

"Forget it. You can just hang your head out the window if you're going to be sick."

I got the window down just in time.

I could hear Dan in the bedroom, changing clothes, while I hugged the toilet in the bathroom down the hall. I'd barely made it up the steps before vomiting again. When dry heaves set in, I looked into the toilet bowl and screamed. The water was blood red, with little chunks that looked like clots.

"I'm throwing up blood!" I yelled, terrified as only someone as drunk as I was can be.

Dan appeared in the doorway, fresh T-shirt and jeans on, and looked down at me. "It's not blood," he said, rolling his eyes. "It's cherries." With that he turned and clunked down the stairs. I heard the front door slam, and he was gone.

Still thoroughly pissed, I collapsed into bed and passed out.

The next morning I carefully made my way downstairs. I was surprised to find Dan asleep on the couch, even more surprised that he was alone. I trudged to the kitchen in search of coffee. My stomach felt terrible, my head worse. As for the night before, I only wanted to forget it.

I was just sitting down with my first cup when Dan came into the kitchen in his boxer shorts. I hadn't had the nerve to look at myself in the mirror that morning, but whatever I looked like, it was hard to imagine myself looking worse than Dan.

"Morning," I mumbled.

Dan said nothing as he poured a mug of steaming coffee. We sat in silence for a long time. He was still in his clothes from the night before, and he looked as bad as I felt.

"Well, how was the bartender?" I asked, feeling catty. I felt I had earned it.

Dan stared at me as if I had just run my finger up my nose to the second knuckle.

"What, you don't want to brag? Lord it over me that you slept with a porn star? I'm surprised," I said.

"Shut up, Brian. Just shut up."

"No, I want to hear all about it. Was he as hot as in the movies? Did he fuck you with that huge cock? Or did you turn him over and do him? What happened?"

"He's dead," Dan said.

"What?"

"He crashed his car into a telephone pole on Monroe Drive. We were going to meet at the Cove after I brought you home. By the time I got there, the police and ambulances were already there. I saw his car, but he was…they had already taken him away. One of the policemen was talking about it. He said…he said the body was pretty torn up."

"Those fucking shooters," I mumbled under my breath.

"We weren't drinking them, you idiot." Dan said, rolling his eyes at me. "Not after the first few, anyway. We were pouring ours out while you sucked them down," he added disdainfully.

My head pounded. While I was puking my guts out and cursing the porn-star bartender, he had crashed his car and died.

It wasn't long after that night that I left Dan and found a place of my own. The bartender's death had ended our relationship—Dan blamed me, I think, for making them drive separately that night.

I, on the other hand, learned I was not an open-marriage kind of guy.

As for the bartender? Well, he was the catalyst that made me realize I had to get a backbone—which is still a work in progress. I didn't even know him, but his death gave me the push I needed to extract myself from a bad situation with Dan and taught me I could expect—and get—more from my relationships.

Death can change you sometimes.

Years later, as I was trawling through one of those news groups on the Internet, the ones with the pictures of naked men, I came across an old studio shot of the bartender. There he was, in his '70s haircut and clone mustache, holding his erect dick at the base, teasing the camera and the viewer—forever beautiful, forever horny. I wondered how many men would look at him and desire him, as Dan had, and how many men knew how, on a hot summer night, he died.

Roosters at the Seashore
by Michael A. White

Palm Beach County, Florida: "Air Force Beach" cum MacArthur Park. At times I would venture into the dunes to pee and be startled by lone individuals under the sea grapes. I was never sure if it was against dune etiquette to urinate, but since so many other bodily fluids were spilled there, I did. Sorry guys.

The beach attracted every ilk of sunbather. There was a nude section, a straight section—the straight section is always closest to the parking lot; they just drag their playpens, strollers, sporting equipment, coolers, cheese puffs, portable televisions, and nacho chips to the first hint of sand, drop it all, and collapse—and a gay section. The gay beach was not the farthest from the parking lot—that was "Birthday Suit Beach"—but it was still a good walk, which created a perfect opportunity for us to parade in new swimwear or beach attire.

Anyway, this is supposed to be a bar story. And it is. A bar on a field trip. Roosters, a local West Palm Beach bar would, on Sundays, pack up rainbow flags, tremendous drink coolers, banners, and a menagerie of staff and road trip to the beach. So on Sunday mornings my husband and I would—as any self-respecting faggot did—head to the shore and wait for the bar. It was like waiting for the circus.

The first sign of the troupe was always the oversized drink coolers carried by a caravan of beautiful bar backs, lead by the (at the time) oversized bar manager. Next came the sawhorses and plywood for the impromptu bar. The most stirring sight was the parachute. Yes, parachute. Not strung up to form a circus tent but spread out to make a dance floor. Rainbow flags and jewel-tone streamers were affixed to poles and positioned around the perimeter of the chute in case anyone had the slightest doubt about this being ground zero for a gay gala.

The music arrived next. A tanned beauty boy sauntered up the beach toting a portable stereo the size of a compact car. Once the music began to pound, the yellow-and-orange parachute became a crowded, sand-free orgy of movement. (I've always been intrigued by movie scenes in which people are rolling around in the sand, tongues probing mouths, peckers probing elsewhere. I have to go home if I get sand in my tanning oil or between my toes; sand in my ass crack is not a cock-lifting thought. And, admit it, the old adage "I'm going to pound sand up your ass" is an unsettling thought for many of you.)

Roosters at the beach always attracted a colorful coterie. If you have not observed two hairy guys with full beards walking down the beach in fuzzy pink bathrobes and flip-flops, only to arrive and change into patent-leather flats and reveal that beneath their bright pink chenille robes are even brighter pink lady's bikinis, then you haven't lived. Let's just say it creates a deeper respect for depilatories. (I won't even start with the feathered headpieces.) And, of course, the muscle boys! My fantasies are still haunted by those bench-pressing beauties. Every week it looked as if a massive, billowing white cloud descended from the brilliant blue Florida sky, settled its edge on the beach, and let the gods step forth. Watching them shake their bubble butts to the beat was more intoxicating than even the spiked punch dispensed from the sawhorses. There was also the obligatory Truman Capote look-alike, with boa and wide-brimmed hat; the guy who arrived so drunk you wondered how he could get from his house to his car, let alone to the beach; and several men who went nude despite being beyond the realm of Birthday Suit Beach. (The ones you want to go nude never do. The ones that do? Well...they provide inspiration to work out and watch what you eat.)

My lover and I rested on our queen-size bedsheet, with more towels than the linens department at Macy's, our bodies in precise alignment with the sun. My lover had suntan positioning down to a science. We shifted every few minutes, on his command, as the sun meandered west.

The music thumped, and bodies bumped, and off in the Atlantic, hurricane Gloria humped. (The National Weather Center should hire a coastal queen to name hurricanes instead of some Midwesterner compelled to use the names of his near and dear. Just imagine: Antoine, Bette, Courbet, Dirk, Erte, Fred. OK, I'm from the Midwest, and Fred is a relative.) We knew Gloria was coming, but we'd been told by the local news that she was no threat to South Florida, that she would hit farther north. Little did we know, hurricanes sometimes create tidal surges by pushing down on the water...or something like that.

My lover and I by this time had shifted parallel to the shoreline in our quest for perfect sun alignment. I, always getting the left side of the bed, was closest to the shore. I had reached a blissful state of near sleep brought about by too much sun, too much liquor, and a whole lot of love. My lover rested on his elbow, smoking, gazing at the turquoise waters off of Palm Beach.

"Oh, my God," he said.

Now, I live in constant fear of nature. Give me cement.

Give me chlorinated water. Give me sticks of dynamite to hurl into the ocean to ensure all sea life in the vicinity of my legs is either dead or moved to calmer waters. At his exclamation my first thought was that a spider crab—the beach is fraught with them—was perched on the edge of our beach blanket, ready to skitter onto my face.

I immediately scooted toward my lover and covered my eyes to protect myself from whatever creature it was that planned to attack me.

The wave hit me full in the face.

The wall of water rolled me over my lover and pushed him, me, sheets, towels, beach bag, shoes, umbrella, sunglasses, books, magazines, lotions, beverages, and cigarettes toward the dunes. Completely submerged, I rolled up the beach. I tried to stand, but the surge held me down, until, suddenly, the ocean stopped moving. I spit sea water from my lungs, planted my feet deep in the sand still covered with three feet of water, and wondered what the hell happened.

The beach was completely submerged, but everyone appeared to be OK. Everything that could float was floating—coolers, a straw hat, apparel billowing like jelly fish. The parachute was nowhere in sight. It looked like a cruise liner had sunk. Our party had become flotsam.

And then, having crashed the party, Gloria decided to leave.

I felt water tug at my legs and, with horror, realized that our belongings were being sucked out to sea. "The car keys!" I screamed to my lover. "Where are the car keys?" I splashed around looking for my shorts. I spotted the corner of one of our towels protruding from the sand, and deeper panic hit as I realized the wave had buried items in the sand.

A few quick-thinking lads picked up anything they could grab and hurled it toward the dunes. And the people on the dunes grabbed the items and pitched them to even higher ground. It became an inspiring, impromptu rescue effort.

As the last of the water pooled on the beach or filtered back to the ocean, we spotted other items buried by the surge. I noticed the tip of my shoe and then my shorts burrowed alongside. At least we could get into our car and drive home.

The bar manager discovered the parachute, and he and his bar backs tugged it from the sand.

I looked seaward. Would it come back?

It never did.

Here's the bitter part: After the tidal surge the state of Florida closed the park for "improvements." The entrance was turned into a half-mile boardwalk. Park rangers were given ATV's to zoom around the park on, in order to ensure that everything was to the letter of the law. (I have never seen a state with so little revenue invest so much money to make sure no one shows a butt cheek or pee-pee.)

Even worse, the surge that smashed the beach that day came at a time when our community was deeply ravaged by another storm—disease. The great wave felt like a kick when we were down.

But Roosters is still open, boys. And still one of the nicest places in West Palm Beach to sit and have a drink. Sure, the tone has changed a little—it doesn't risk the beach anymore—but it's still there. And so are we. The survivors.

Backroom News
by Wayne Hoffman

He didn't say a word to me. Just a quick leer through his mirrored sunglasses and a forceful hand on my shoulder pushing me down, and I was on my knees unbuckling his belt.

He didn't whisper words of encouragement or bark commands as I sucked his dick. He just leaned back against a big black motorcycle, one hand holding his half-burned cigar, the other gripping a shot glass of gin or scotch or whatever it is that tough guys drink.

I had come to Chicago for two reasons: a journalists' conference by day and backroom action by night. And I'd had more than my fill of the first. I kept sucking, unsure if he was even looking at me—or if he could see anything at all, wearing sunglasses in such a dark room.

But then the noise started to build. A circle of men behind us egged on a hungry bottom with lines like "Yeah, suck that dick!" and "You like that dick, don't you?" that they had surely heard in some porn movie. A man bound and hooded in latex was rattling against his cage nearby. And closer to the entrance, a gaggle of queens (in leather, yes, but queens) chitchatted loudly, ignoring the backroom etiquette they should have learned from Miss Manners—if only Miss Manners covered the really important things.

I tried to tune it all out, focusing on my cigar daddy, who, if he seemed aloof and indifferent, had a brickbat of an erection that said otherwise. But he was apparently having a harder time ignoring our neighbors' conversation. He put his hand on my shoulder again—this time to stop me—took off his sunglasses, and looked down to utter his first words to me, gravely serious: "The princess is dead."

I had already heard the news, of course, that Princess Diana had been killed in a car accident in Paris. I looked up. "I know," I said gently, and got back to work, knowing I had to finish him off quickly, before the grief overwhelmed him.

I admit I had been caught up in the excitement of royal tragedy myself only an hour earlier. I had arrived at the Cell Block with a group of people from the conference and met up with an old friend from Chicago, Bill, who told me the news. He had only heard bits and pieces on the radio on the way over in a taxi, but we could piece together enough to get the basic story: a car accident, possibly fatal.

As journalists, however, we wanted details. Up front in the bar it was hard to talk, since the music was loud and a bunch of bears was hawking some porno video they were playing on the TV screens.

So a few of us headed into the back bar (leather required), where the TVs showed a video of fisting and shaving that looked about as erotic as a gym-class hygiene film. I leaned over the bar and asked the bartender if he could switch on CNN for a moment so we could hear about Diana. He didn't deign to answer.

So we were left to gather details from other customers as best we could. We split up to cover more territory.

Bill stood up front and asked his local bear pals for information as they walked in, hoping those who arrived later would have more recent information from more recent taxi rides and could confirm or deny the rumors of the princess's death. But they seemed more interested in the porn than the accident. Andy, a writer from North Carolina, stood in the back bar, too overwhelmed to do proper investigations. It was his first time in a leather bar; he'd had to borrow leather suspenders—far too large for his skinny 20-something frame—to get past the gatekeeper, and he wasn't quite prepared for what he found. The videos had him mesmerized (or scared), and a stocky, cigar-chomping leatherman with the bushiest walrus mustache in the Windy City kept him more than amply distracted simply by tweaking Andy's nipples and leering with a hard stare. When I passed and asked if he'd heard anything new, Andy was barely able to muster a nod of recognition.

Jack, a muscle-bound editor from Michigan, had started out with strong resolve, talking to bartenders, strangers by the dance floor, and the doorman, trying to piece together more certain information. But when I checked on him a few minutes later, he was busy trying to set up an orgy in his hotel room. Whatever had happened in Paris, Jack's priorities in Chicago lay elsewhere.

It was up to me to get the lowdown. So I stripped off the T-shirt under my leather vest and headed into the back room.

First I headed to a tall man in a leather jacket, with a shaved head and gray goatee, leaning against the chain-link spider web stretched across the middle of the room. He liked having his tits chewed on, and I was happy to oblige, in exchange for vital information. I chewed away, jerking his cock through the open fly of his 501s, the chain web jangling against itself in an increasing rhythm, until he came in my hand. He offered me the hanky from his pocket to clean up, and I asked him—while his butch defenses were down—what he'd heard about Princess Diana. "There was an accident," he confirmed, "but that's all I know." Over in the corner I spied the couple I had met the night before at the Ram, a dirty bookstore across the street. Both were short, dark, and bearded, in their 40s, from Memphis or Louisville or somewhere with an accent. I could still picture them covering my beard with their loads the previous night, and it wasn't long before I had the same pleasure again. After getting them off for the second time in 24 hours, I figured we were nearly kin, so I asked what they'd heard. The driver's dead, they told me with a twang, but they didn't know about Diana. "I sure hope she's all right," the older one said with visible concern, allowing himself some vulnerability for a moment. I licked my lips and nodded.

I spotted the jackpot over by the door: John, who had come up from Florida with his lover Rick, a journalist whom I'd met at the previous year's conference. John and I had been making eyes throughout the day's workshops and plenary sessions. He was uncomfortable flirting with Rick around, but in the backroom it was just me and John, all 6 feet 4 inches of him. I knew he'd know everything, and I knew I'd have fun getting it out of him. After a long spell of kissing and a slow and deliberate blow job, he shot all over my vest as I held onto his long, lean thighs. Before he was even done buckling up, I asked what he knew. "The driver is dead," he said. "And so is Diana. The paparazzi killed them. Drove them right into a concrete wall in the middle of a tunnel."

I knew enough facts to file a report and decided to head back up front to broadcast my findings to my colleagues from the conference. But before I could leave the back room, I spotted the man with mirrored shades leaning against the motorcycle.

They can wait a few more minutes, I decided. The princess may be dead, but this queen is still horny.

Beasts in the Burbs
by Mark C. Abbott

The Griffon, in sleepy, middle-class Sanlando Springs, is my favorite watering hole when I get a free evening on visits to my family in Central Florida. Unlike most big-city gay bars, people will actually talk with you there. It's quiet and small enough to be friendly and mood-lit at every hour. The long L-shaped bar is perfect for direct eye contact if you sit on the bar's shorter leg; otherwise, there's always the mirror behind the bottles. Best of all, the bartenders will chat you up if no one else will, and they've been known to make introductions—newcomers to regulars—after an appropriate interview to screen for pathologies. All in all, the Griffon is a cozy place where people can be themselves and trust that others likewise are relaxed.

Some of the regulars are very much so, arriving almost every night around the same time and staying the same number of hours or drinks, depending on how you count the traffic. They even check in before going on a date or vacation to keep abreast of their mates' latest news, latest moves, and latest cruise. It's a place where everyone knows your name if you show up enough.

The past couple years I've gotten there maybe once or twice a year for a long weekend. The barkeeps and a few regulars rec-

ognize me and often recall the last time we chatted: movies, va-
cations, outrageous parties we've attended or (more usually)
heard tell of, episodes of intense stress or weirdness or joy or
love. Oprah's lineup has nothing on what gay men can dish up,
just from their own biographies, especially those impromptu
works of fiction known as bar bios, where everyone is a doctor,
producer, or black-sheep heir to the family's citrus fortune. Most
of the time at the Griffon, though, it's laughs and local gossip.

The night of my first thirsty foray to the Griffon in some
time, I sat near a familiar face on the long leg of the L-shaped
bar. A familiar face, Ronny, commanded the corner, his usual
place. (He's an every night man.) He didn't place me at first,
but he's a motormouth and will talk to anyone. Happily, he
has a wonderful sense of humor, can talk about almost anything, and is easy on the eyes: long blond hair, bright blue
peepers, tall and slender. Jeepers! Still, a walk through the
marshes of his mind will barely get your toes wet.

Mostly he spoke with his buddy Erasmus, a swarthy, dark-
haired, muscular beauty whose ancestors must have built pyra-
mids somewhere, maybe Peru. Erasmus, or Raz, also had his
dog, Tequila, with him. Raz breeds canines, and this brindle
boxer, four weeks pregnant, was as sweet, friendly, and well-
behaved a pooch as there ever was. She loved the scent of my
brother's German shepherd on my sandals—or maybe the ath-
lete's foot ointment I used. Who knows? There's no account-
ing for doggie tastes.

Winnie the bartender looked up, just as I did, when a rather
loud and slurry question rang out: "Whattaya serve a straight man
in here?" Some guy by the video games, clear at the other end,
who sounded already smashed. Winnie served him a beer, and all
was quiet again, except Ronny recounting his day's adventures.

Absorbed as he was with several admirers, Ron paid scant

attention to me, so my gaze drifted to the mirror, mostly to check out how a handsome 25-year-old was dealing with the wiry lawn-service guy old enough to be his father.

Then the self-declared straight man rose from his seat, mouth agape, shirt exploding from his trousers, and stumbled toward the door. Rounding the L, he almost stepped on Tequila, asleep at her master's feet, slurring "I don't have anything against you ho-mo-sexshuls, but dontcha know what you're doing is wrong? Have you ever thought about what God thinks o' what you're doin'? Have ya ever had a talk with your maker?"

Rural Florida's finest: Bible-thumping trailer trash.

I'll give the motormouth all honor and credit because Ronny sure knew what to say next: "Well, we don't have anything against you, either. Just want to be free and happy, same as you. And I'm on very good terms with my creator, thank you, since He made me how I am."

"But it's wrong in the eyes of the Lord!"

"Don't get me started, fella. You're dealing with a certified, sanctified, Southern Baptist from Tidewater, Virginia., the buckle of the Bible Belt! And don't the Bible say, 'Judge not, lest ye be judged?' "

"But what're ya gonna do come Judgment Day?"

"That'll be between me and God. You *do* know you're in a gay bar, don't you?"

"You're headed down the same road as that bastard Cunanan."

"Cunanan was a sicko, a prostitute, for Pete's sake. Not much at all like us here. We're all pretty average guys who just happen to keep falling in love with men. And none of us knew Andrew Cunanan. Except maybe this fella here, who was a whore in L.A." Ronny points and turns to me, redirecting the sot.

"You were a prostitute? In Californey? And knew that murderer?"

Now, I'm crowding age 50—lots of gray hair, several chins, and more bulges at the waistline than a pony keg. Still, I suppose it's remotely plausible that I look like an aged hustler— the boyish good looks are not totally smothered by gravity's ravages, especially to someone obviously plowed and on a mission to evangelize.

But I've never been one to rise to the bait of saving and sin hating, especially when peddled by folks with too much fire— or firewater—in them. Astonished at Ronny's ploy and half laughing at how smoothly he'd passed me the ball, I decided to feint. "L.A.?" I said. "Naw, I'm from around here. Never spent much time in Californey." Confused, the drunk turned away— toward the dog, who by now was all ears, on all fours, with Raz firmly holding her chain. The sot stared. "Ya don't mean to tell me ya jump dawgs, do ya? Ya don't hump male dawgs, I hope!"

"Well, not the kind you're thinking of," sang out a bearded guy from the tables almost in the next room, to general laughter.

"Dontcha all just go home with each other? Or do ya take a dumb beast home with ya both and jump it too?"

"No, most often we don't leave with anyone," replied the beard. "And not by choice! That's just how it goes. Most nights we sit home and beat it, just like you."

The drunk staggered and slowly, inadvertently, lurched toward Tequila.

On her best behavior, Tequila backed up a bit and stared him down, ears flat against her head, ready for anything. He made another, jerkier move—to pet? to strike?—and she voiced her distress. Not a growl or a whimper exactly, but something in-between. Raz's gaze matched Tequila's, and for a moment he looked as if he might just turn her loose to do her worst.

"Don't provoke her," warned the beard.

"Ya don't do dawgs; ya don't do each other. You must be

lez-bee-yuns," said the souse, wheeling to face the bearded man. It was his last loud remark: Winnie and the beard were in his face—almost touching tummies—calmly telling him his visit was over; it was time to leave; he'd insulted everyone; and he'd better get going before they called the cops. My brother's cell phone was in my pants pocket, and I fingered the keypad, ready to call in the cavalry. But there was no need. Winnie and the beard escorted the drunk outside with little resistance.

Tequila's parting shot was to turn her bum to the guy and glance over her rump as he was shepherded out the door. *Jump this, asshole!* her stance seemed to say.

Good doggie.

Once they'd returned from the front, Winnie and the bearded guy—World's Hairiest Lesbian, one gal proclaimed him—got a round of applause, and the dozen or so customers burst into conversation. We tried to diagnose the source of the trouble, finally settling on horror stories from the time of Anita Bryant that had conditioned rubes and fundamentalists to expect no-holds-barred orgies in every gay venue, at any hour of day or night—Sodom at the Sidetrack Tap, right here in River City.

The disappointment of finding a rather quiet, ordinary group of folks just sitting and talking must've been a shock to someone who'd gone forth to do the Lord's work. Worse still, no one had paid him much attention until he got loaded and loud and declared himself an outsider. He must have been disappointed by how dull we were.

"Maybe we should've told him Tequila is the pit bull on the news, the one that tore up that lady, out on parole for the weekend. That woulda put the fear of the Lord in him," surmised Ronny, his last words on the night's main event.

As always, I enjoyed my night at the Griffon. It's a nice place. But I guess it's not for everyone.

Adventure at the Phoenix
by Blaise Bulot

Although it was nearly midnight when Hipolyte entered the Phoenix on Elysian Fields, there were only a handful of patrons downstairs: one leaning over the pool table with a provocative tear in the seat of his Levis, two fatties at the bar, and one getting his boots shined by a beefy apparition in a black leather harness.

Hipolyte headed straight for the toilet—he had to go fierce—but when he got there a guy came out and said, "Hey man, don' go in dere. Ah jus' haid a good dump an' almos' set da smoke detector off." Hipolyte checked anyway. But a throne queen had already perched on the stool, probably for hours.

He headed for the bathroom upstairs, which was darker than the Stygian realm. In contrast to the lower bar, the upstairs bar was packed. Shadowy figures crowded the murky gloom. Some of the shapes were lighter than others, and they were in various states of undress. Hipolyte wore only a vest and his Daisy Dukes. Nothing underneath.

There was not a glimmer of light in the toilet. With his hands in front of him, he groped his way into the darkness. Before he even reached the stall, though, strange hands were all over him. Off came the vest. Down went the cutoffs. His cock was in something warm and moist. A mouth or an arse-hole?

He felt down in front of him and touched a head of curly hair—so it must have been a mouth.

Hipolyte couldn't find his vest, so he reached down to pull his cutoffs up. They wouldn't budge. He tugged harder and still couldn't pull them up. Bent over like he was, he was a target for finger fucking or worse. Somebody seized the opportunity. Hipolyte ignored it and felt around on the sticky floor, felt a sneaker. Somebody was standing on his pants. Three fingers in now. He pushed at the foot, but it didn't move. He pulled harder at his cutoffs. *R-r-r-ip.* A sickening sound. *Goodness me,* he thought. *Ah'm in real trouble now.* Hipolyte finally got his Daisy Dukes up and zipped. But he was still hanging out. It was a big rip.

He pulled his shorts together and went and sat on the picnic table pushed under the eaves and tried to hide the rip—but it didn't work. In no time at all, other hands found it. Fingers fumbled through the tear, into his crotch, up his gee-gee. Hands pulled off the torn cutoffs.

Hipolyte gave in. He turned over on the picnic table—onto his hands and knees, his naked biscuits in the air, his pearly gates spread wide. A deft and insistent finger probed his rosebud. The finger was replaced by a flickering tongue. *Someone sure is tossing my salad,* Hipolyte thought. The tongue pushed into his wazoo deeper and deeper. Then the hot tongue was replaced by something *very* cold. Hipolyte whooped and jerked. Giggles all around. Some fiend was fingering ice cubes out of drinks and pushing them up Hipolyte's nooky. One after another. Hipolyte twisted this way and that and moaned. More giggles.

"Loves it, don' ya'll?" a voice asked.

But then, all of a sudden, Hipolyte had to take a crap real bad. Even worse than before. He grabbed his Daisy Dukes and rushed to the toilet downstairs. Full. The throne queen was still there. He begged her to vacate, but all she did was laugh and moisten her lips with her tongue.

He ran out the front door—you know, that tight-arse sort of run when you don't think you're going to make it—shorts in hand. He made it to the neutral ground and squatted behind a big oleander bush. He blasted away like a burst fire hydrant. Luckily, there is not much traffic on Elysian Fields that late. He found a page from the *Times-Picayune* caught under the bush and tried to wipe himself. Hipolyte wondered, *Do journalists mind what sometimes happens to their work?* But he ran out of paper. Still dripping. Running down his leg. All over his sneakers.

Someone had followed him out, though. Hipolyte didn't bother looking to see who cuz whoever it was kneeled down and lapped him off, completing his adventure at the Phoenix. Did a very thorough job.

Night Town
by Randy Clark

One night McQueen got so drunk that on our way home
he threw up on the jade plants at the edge of the old people's
apartments around the corner from the bar. Most of the time
none of us got that wasted, and for many months afterward we
teased him about jade plants. Usually, however, our days did
end at that bar. In a small town your options are limited. Night
Town, for us, was that single gay bar by the bus station, the
streets around it, and sometimes the other bars that came and
went on the outskirts of town.

Another option, if you wanted to call it that, was to go beneath the wharf at a nearby beach. It was a cruising ground,
but you could hardly call it anonymous when most of the people who went there were people you saw every day. I avoided it; McQueen went there often. The rumor was that there
was a brass plaque in his honor attached to one of the pylons.
Some people believed it was really there.

People believed the most ridiculous rumors and told them as
gospel along with other, more plausible tales. That too was part
of living in a small town. Confronted with a story about his sex
life, McQueen had one of two answers: Either he would wave
his hand and dismissively say, "It's all true," or he would shout,

"Lies! Lies! It's all lies! Well, *that* part is true, but the rest is lies!" McQueen taught me how to cope with the gossip.

Gossip also had it that Howard and I were lovers. Howard was a friend from the radio station where I worked and my best friend in daily life. Usually we were together at the bar; often we had dinner together; and we particularly enjoyed going to movie revivals at the small theater over near the freeway. Howard had a crush on the theater's manager. Howard had crushes on a number of men, most of them straight, all of them unavailable. This is a bad habit for a gay man to have, but I could sympathize. Howard spent a lot of time and energy on these young men. Eventually, in frustration, he would return to the beach and the wharf.

Howard introduced me to McQueen. During the summer of '83 I had noticed a newcomer to the bar, a slim blond who always looked disheveled—not as if his clothes weren't clean but as if he'd been through the drier with them. The clothes were always black and white. One night he showed up while Howard and I were sitting there, and I learned they knew each other from before I had even moved to town. (I had arrived in '82.) McQueen had gone to the city to pursue a love affair, then returned when that fell apart. At first I was interested in him, but he didn't return the interest. He had a crush on Howard, also unrequited. This low-temperature triangle was one the gossips never noticed. It didn't prevent us from becoming fast friends.

Howard was tall and dignified, with dark hair and Joan Crawford eyebrows. He wore a World War II airman's jacket. Its pockets always contained a corkscrew, rolling papers, and a condom. His humor was dry. He called the town "Hairy Palms, Calif."

Night Town. Night after night we sat there nursing our

cocktails, chatting, and watching the crowd. Most of the faces were familiar. When the door opened, heads turned to see if it was someone new. Newcomers got a lot of attention.

It wasn't until I had left town and returned for a visit that I noticed no one in town ever greeted you with, "What's new?" They assumed nothing was.

The bar's decor changed gradually over time but always there was a vaguely Polynesian theme. Over the bar was a large cloth mural of drummers and a woman hula dancer who was mysteriously missing one arm. Two light boxes with stained glass showed a surfer and flamingos. In the background was a volcano. On the back wall were murals of palm trees and sand—until they knocked the wall out and turned the storeroom into a dance floor. When they knocked out the wall, the toilets moved to the rear of the dance floor: just two one-seat rooms, despite the crowds on weekends, which got worse when young straight people in town decided it was cool to go to a gay bar, even though a lot of them didn't want to deal with the actual gay people inside it. Management lined the toilet rooms with sheet metal because of vandalism. If you found soap or paper towels, you were lucky.

The walls of the bar also had tiki masks, which fortunately disappeared over time. One of the masks was broken during a bar fight. After the straight guy swinging punches had been ejected from the bar, McQueen looked at the pieces of the mask and said, "Every cloud has a silver lining."

The music never changed. Half a dozen early '80s tapes played repeatedly. Whether you liked them or not, the songs sunk into your head. Videotape wears out, but these tapes lasted forever. The bar is still playing them.

The nicest part of the bar was the bay window facing the street, with a table in it. We called it the office. On weekends

Night Town began as early as 4:30 in the afternoon, when the
bar opened. We sat in the office and watched the boys on the
sidewalk. In a beach town the view is often good. Some of the
local boys became known by sight: the long-haired skate-
boarder we nicknamed Metallica, the bicycling waiter with a
limp but a great butt, the kid in the baseball cap who loitered
outside the bar and who finally turned 21 and joined us inside
as we had expected he would. Most of the faces outside were
as familiar as the faces inside, but they were more intriguing.

The other good part of the bar was its employees. Gable was
handsome and friendly and poured generous drinks. "He's trying to kill me!" Howard would exclaim. Crewes, the manager, became a personal friend and invited us to parties on the
Fourth of July and Halloween at the large Victorian house he
shared with several others. But when he wasn't bartending, he
kept a low profile.

Toward the end of the evening, McQueen would get tired
of it all and announce, "I'm only 13, officer, and I just want to
go home." Sometimes it was, "I'm only 13, and my dad's
going to kill me!" Once he and some friends really were
stopped by the police, coming home not very sober from one
of the edge-of-town bars. As I recall, McQueen was standing
out of the sun roof. Luckily, the car's driver recognized the pa-
trolman—they had met at a bathhouse. The officer tore up the
citation and warned the boys to tone it down.

From time to time McQueen would appear in drag, not just
on Halloween but on random nights as well. He had two dis-
tinct styles: one respectable and upper-class, the other a mix of
cycle slut and Lolita.

Through McQueen I met McDaniel, who dressed up even
more often than McQueen and in outfits of striking originali-
ty. McDaniel was part Irish but mostly Native American. Out

of drag he was handsome. In drag he was feisty and got into
fights more often than any of my other friends. Once or twice
I was tempted to swing at him myself. But usually we were in
agreement. For instance, there was a confused man who made
a habit of showing up at the bar, butting into conversations,
and harassing people about being gay. The first time we saw
him, he joined the office table uninvited. When he started asking why we didn't believe being gay was wrong, McQueen
lost no time in saying, "You're excused." The man didn't get
it. McQueen persisted: "You're excused now. You can leave
this table. I think you should." He didn't. McDaniel and I slid
off our bar stools and told him he wasn't welcome. The only
threat was in our posture, but he did go out the door. Immediately afterward a woman came over to us and objected, saying, "You were going to hit him!" "No, we weren't," we said.
"You were going to hit him," she insisted.

When McQueen and McDaniel dressed up together, things
could get out of hand. One night McQueen had too much to
drink, didn't want to walk through the crowd, and became indignant when McDaniel refused to tell the cab to come to the
alley in back of the bar. Another night I drove the two of them
home, both wearing dresses and heels. When McQueen got out
of my car in front of his apartment, he fell so rapidly that from
inside the car, it looked like he had simply disappeared. Instead
of rushing to help, McDaniel and I collapsed in laughter.

On yet another night McQueen dressed in his scariest outfit: red pumps, fake snakeskin capri pants ("They're real ure-
thane," he told everyone), camisole over rubber tits, cat-eye
glasses, and a curly black wig with a bow in it. Dressed this
way, he was hit on by a straight guy in a letter jacket. The
straight guy took McQueen to his apartment, where he fon-
dled the tits. "You know those aren't real," McQueen said. "I

don't care," the straight guy replied. Then his housemates showed up and wanted him for something, banging on his bedroom door, so he and McQueen fled out the window. Mc-Queen twisted his ankle in the process. They limped over to McQueen's apartment, where they finished fooling around. The next morning McQueen discovered the straight guy had stolen a pair of sunglasses.

Howard's and my adventures were usually less colorful. My favorite adventure of Howard's is the night he picked up a boy who was camping on the beach. The boy had seemed eager, but when they got to Howard's place, he didn't want to put out. Indignant, Howard drove him back to the beach and abandoned him. "And he'd been with some other queen already," Howard grumbled. "I know the smell of Crabtree & Evelyn."

And as for me? I didn't care for outdoor cruising, so I waited in the bar, watching for an opportunity, feeling left out more often than not. I was one of the ones who watched the front door. Most of the time I wanted to meet a man who would be a lover, but I went through phases where I wanted to be on my own, and a one-night arrangement would have suited me just fine. On two occasions men said they wanted to be lovers with me but wanted me to commit to a relationship before they would have sex. I thought they were overly optimistic. I've never encountered that expectation anywhere else in the gay world.

Once in a while I had better luck than usual. There was the traveler from Greece who offered me a massage and then, to my pleasant surprise, hung around for a couple of weeks. There was the Irish-looking kid who said he was straight when I met him at a party but slipped into the men's room with me so we could piss together and later went home with me. There was the first man I tied up; we were together half a year. There was…well, there were others.

There was also the time I went home with a friend of Mc-Daniel's, one of Crewes's housemates who'd been chasing me for a couple of weeks. I liked him but wasn't that interested because I was going through one of my romance phases, and this was not a romance situation. But after an evening at an edge-of-town bar, I agreed to go back to his place. We fooled around on his bed for a bit, then he left to use the toilet…and never returned. I lay there feeling increasingly foolish and finally climbed out his window and drove home. I later learned that he'd passed out in a hallway.

Most nights, though, we would look around Night Town and see what we'd seen before and decide not to bother. Once the four of us were there until closing. Afterward there was the usual crowd of about 40 men milling about outside the bar because they wanted to go home with someone but not with anyone there. McQueen looked at this spectacle and exclaimed, "Midnight, all alone on the pavement!"

We knew a couple who lived in the hills above town. Every summer they threw a mammoth pool party and barbecue. The four of us went and swam and drank and ate. Someone gave us a lift back to town in the back of their panel truck. Seeing the truck, McQueen immediately went into a woman-behind-bars routine. Howard was fairly glazed and appreciated the humor. In the dim light neither of them noticed that McDaniel was getting inside my clothes. I didn't stop him. I took him home. We were fuck buddies from that night on for the next couple of years.

McQueen moved in with McDaniel, who not long afterward was arrested because he'd "borrowed" a boyfriend's credit card, and the boyfriend's lover got jealous and busted him. When McQueen went to visit McDaniel in jail, the first words he said were, "You look *horrible* in orange!" The charge was minor, and the sentence was only a few weeks, but the stories were huge: that the house McQueen and McDaniel lived in was "raided," for what it was never clear ("They released all the teenagers I had chained up in the basement," one house-mate sarcastically complained); and that when the cops went into McDaniel's house, they found a closet full of $10,000 evening gowns ("I wish I'd known," said McQueen).

McDaniel introduced me to Leigh, who was tall and from the Northwest. Leigh got his lesson in the town's smallness the first week he arrived. He had spent the night with the same housemate of Crewes's who had once passed out on me. A few afternoons later he was at the bar and Crewes, working there, asked if he was seeing anyone. No, Leigh said, but he had gone home with someone a few nights before...and Crewes ex-claimed, "Oh, that was you!"

Leigh and I got along so well, so quickly, that at first I thought we were going to be a romantic pair. We did have friendly sex a couple of times but wound up as friends instead.

Once Howard, McQueen, and I were sitting at the bar, and one of the bartenders said, "Look at the three of you. If one of you left, what would happen? Then I guess there'd be two of you." As it happened, Howard was the first to leave town, then McQueen moved to the city, and I longed to follow. Mc-Daniel moved up there as well, and so did Leigh. For a while there was only one of me. Finally I moved too.

Not long before my friends left town, the bar instigated a cover fee on weekends. Officially this was to pay the DJs. In reality it was to keep out customers with little money. (Not that any of us had much money in those years.) The owner of the bar assured all the regulars that we wouldn't have to pay the cover, and he did indeed draw up a guest list. Eventually, though, and inevitably, he hired a doorman who didn't know us. I was sitting at the office table when McQueen arrived for the evening. The doorman tried to charge him. Sweeping one hand over his head, McQueen sailed past saying, "Oh, darling, you simply *must* be out of your mind!"

Fifteen years later the five of us live in the city. We are still friends, though we don't see each other as often as we used to, and we are never together all at once, the way we often were in Night Town.

When we see each other we say, "What's new?"

Rocky I, II, III, IV, V
by Chip Livingston

Rocky I

Believing every Friday night is possibly the night, I tan early, go to the gym, work my chest hard. The black-shirt boy must work Saturday nights because I have only seen him on Fridays. The black-shirt boy is why I have taken to going out Fridays. It's a quiet crowd, but it holds possibility.

Saturday nights I go out with friends to the same bar I go to alone on Fridays. Saturday nights are party nights: throw-down, get-drunk, wake-up-with-someone-you're-supposed-to-be-friends-with nights. Somebody-new nights. Friday nights are for dates, dinner, theater, renting movies. I go to Proteus on Friday nights, hating that I appear desperate to the same barmen who serve me Newcastles on Fridays and Absolut on the rocks on Saturdays. I drink alone on Fridays, lingering in the shadows, scanning the door, anticipating his arrival, careful not to get drunk with no friends to depend on for a ride home. On Saturdays I cause cacophony: catcalling, carousing, cruising boys, sweating and shirtless in a dance-floor swarm.

The black-shirt boy was pointed out to me on a Monday—a special event, invitation-only private Proteus party for VIPs and big tippers. Stripper Dan stepped off the go-go box to point out the black-shirt boy as the one who looked past everyone, through everyone, didn't make eye contact. *Kind of short but beautiful. Yes, the most beautiful boy in the bar. Why don't I know him? Why haven't I seen him before?*

Rocky II

Several Fridays later I find myself at the club, sans friends, full of hope. I drink a Newcastle, scan the room, see a vaguely familiar face. A boy in a gray shirt sways on the dance floor. *Is that him? It looks like him, but I'm not sure.* I also wear a gray T-shirt, tucked in beneath a navy blue button-down that I quickly remove and leave with the coat check. I slide the numbered paper into my back pocket. I carry my beer to the dance floor, nonchalantly making my way toward the boy in the other gray shirt. As I get closer, I realize it isn't him. But, whoa, just the same. Same dark hair, longer in the front. Blue eyes, strong mouth, beautiful lips. Great chest. Arms.

Soon we are dancing, getting closer, getting sweaty and suggestive. *A substitute. Like New Coke. Maybe sweeter.* Gray Shirt pulls me to him between songs. "Kiss me," he says, and I kiss him, wondering if the black-shirt boy will come in and think me already coupled. The music starts up again, and I pull Gray Shirt tighter, kiss him deeper. *Joke the black-shirt boy if he can't take a fuck.* Gray Shirt turns out to be Heyward, 20. Another chicken. Quite good in bed and sweet, yes, but I can't imagine him sweeter than the black-shirt boy. I spend the night with Heyward but drive home for breakfast.

Rocky III

"Hey, Chip."

We kiss hello.

"Paul, how are you?" *Why do fags always kiss hello? I'm kind of a handshake guy myself. But when in Greece…*

"What are you doing here? You don't usually come out on Fridays, do you?"

"I have been lately. I'm kind of on a quest."

Paul grins. "Uh-oh. What kind of quest?"

"Let's go outside."

I light a cigarette and lead Paul to the patio.

"I have a huge crush on this guy that comes here on Fridays. The black-shirt boy."

"You're one of the crazies."

"I know, right. Boy crazy. I'm obsessed."

"What do you know about him?"

"Absolutely nothing. Well, I think he's probably trouble." I tell Paul about the black-shirt boy—what I know, anyway, which isn't much. We finish the cigarette and go back inside. I buy a beer. Paul gets an orange juice.

"Not drinking?"

"Driving. But it looks like a drink, right?"

I nod my head. We make our way through the crowd. Near the dance floor I see the black-shirt boy. "That's him. There. Wearing a black shirt again." I point to three guys standing, talking.

"Rocky? That's Rocky, you fool. And he's way married."

"Married?"

"Has a lover. And attitude for days."

"See. I knew he'd be trouble. Introduce me." I follow Paul to the group. *Rocky.* I nudge Paul in the side. "Casually," I add.

Paul first introduces me to Stuart. We make small talk. "Where are you from? What do you do?" I'm nervous and want a cigarette but worry Rocky doesn't smoke. Eventually, Paul starts talking to Rocky, and I turn from Stuart and introduce myself.

"Where are you from?" I ask.

"Oregon. You?"

"Atlanta."

"I hear Atlanta's really nice."

"It's great."

Rocky pulls out a dark brown cigarette. Lights it. A clove. "My boyfriend is moving to Florida." The tangy smell lingers in the air. Sweet. I light a Camel.

A cocktail boy comes through the crowd with a tray over his head. "Can I get you anything?"

Rocky orders a shot of tequila.

I swallow the last of my beer. "A marriage on the rocks."

"A what?"

"An Absolut on the rocks."

Rocky IV

I can't sleep. It is Sunday morning, and I can't sleep. I sit on the floor of my kitchen, leaning against the dishwasher; it hasn't been run in awhile. I can't eat. It's Sunday morning, and I can't eat. I stare at the refrigerator, the Poetry Magnets. I don't write poetry, but I'm writing poetry. Putting together black words on white tiles in lines on the tan refrigerator. I stand up, the word *trouble* in my hands.

Kissing my way back
from your boxers
to your chest. I pause
tracing the scar on your abdomen.
Tasting the story written
permanently on the body.
How many stories have you?
What is your oldest scar?

How did you get this
one I would ask.
You would lie Knife fight.
I say the same of mine.
None of the stories are true
so don't ask.

Rocky you said when I asked your name.
Like the boxer?
Like the road.

Trouble I thought. Trouble
I think, making my way
back to your neck. I want
to bite you so hard
I draw blood. Leave
my mark but I don't.
I nuzzle into your neck
pull my legs up
around you. Sleep
like spoons.

I watched you four
weeks. Wondering when where
how to approach you. Rocky
I know now. Before
it was the black-shirt boy.
Have you seen the
black-shirt boy?
I looked. I
found you, even though
you weren't lost.

Rocky you said when I asked your name.
Like the boxer?
Like the mountains.

I imagine myself watching you
now. Watching us.
I rise above
us floating
looking down. Doesn't look
like trouble now. Looks
like love. From here
I can't feel you against me.
I can only see us
there baby sleeping.
Your body twitches. In dream
I wonder. Or are you
coming to join me?

I throw the word *moist* in the trash can. Then I take the magnetic tile out of the trash and put it in the garbage disposal. Turn on the water, turn on the disposal, listen as the teeth grind and tear, disposing of a word that will never appear in a poem on my fridge. I think about the upcoming Friday. Proteus.

Rocky V

"I'd like to ask you five questions every time I see you."
"What?"
"Can I ask you five questions?"
"Sure, I guess."
"One. Are you a Capricorn?"
"Yes."
"Oh."

"Oh what?"

"Well, question two was to ask what sign you were in case you weren't a Capricorn."

"Hmm. How did you know I was a Capricorn?"

"I didn't. I had a hunch."

"Is that good?"

"I don't know. I don't know anything about Capricorns."

"What sign are you?"

"Cancer. Directly across the chart."

"What does that mean?"

"I'm not sure. That we're compatible."

"More questions?"

"Well, since my number two question is out, and your boyfriend isn't here, which was question number three, maybe my number two question should be, Do you want to dance?"

"Sure, let's get a drink first."

"Absolut on the rocks. No. A Newcastle."

I follow Rocky to the bar, carry my beer to the dance floor. Dance, drink, close my eyes, hope Rocky is watching. We dance, sweat, turn, and dance with others around us. The music slows down, and our drinks empty. Rocky follows me to the bar. I order two Newcastles and a shot of tequila and hand Rocky a beer and the shot. I light a Camel. Rocky drinks the shot without lime or salt, winces, takes out a clove. I light it. Rocky stands against the bar with beer and brown cigarette like a supermodel.

"Super duper," I say.

"What?"

"Nothing."

"You have three questions left."

"Right. Number 3: Can I call you Lucky?"

"Lucky? Why?"

"Everyone calls you Rocky."

"It's my name."

"I think you're good luck."

"You're funny. That's sweet."

"I take that as a yes."

Lucky nods.

"Question four. When did you tell me your boyfriend was moving?"

"He's leaving in two weeks."

"That will be tough." *Is it a statement? Is it a question?*

"Yeah. I'll miss him. We'll split up."

"It sucks when you don't break up but just move away. There's no closure."

"That's life, I guess."

"I left a boyfriend in Atlanta when I moved to Colorado."

"Really?"

"Yeah. He's coming to visit in a week."

"That's cool, I guess." *Is it a question? Is it a statement?*

The music stops. The DJ announces last call.

"Last question?"

He nods, acquiescing.

"Number 5: Why did you tell me your boyfriend was moving?"

Lucky smiles. "Let's dance before they turn the music off."

Five Nights
by Ian-Andrew McKenzie

Night 1

I had hoped for one of my favorite line dances, perhaps "Bayou City Twister" or "County Line," but the Hoedown's DJ introduced "Boot Scoot Boogie," and some friends grabbed me and pulled me with them to the dance floor. It's a simple dance, not challenging, and the song is nothing special. I went through the sequences hoping maybe the next dance would be "Electric Slide," which I can do in reverse, facing everyone else and making lots of eye contact. I wanted to flirt with the other dancers and some spectators.

I like to add a spin in "Boot Scoot Boogie," and it was during one of these spins that I caught him out of the corner of my eye. Tall, blonde, with a goatee, he was very handsome. He looked to be a few inches taller than the man I had recently dated and a bit more rugged as well. He wore a dark leather jacket and held his bottle by the neck as he watched me dance. His attention made me warm, and I wished we were doing a more impressive line dance. At least I knew all the words to the song, allowing me to look at and sing to him. He stood smiling, and when I smiled back he shook his head, as if in disbelief. Suddenly, I was liking "Boot Scoot Boogie" a little bit more.

At the end of the song, I started toward the exit of the dance floor. "Boxcar" was the next dance, a repetitive, jerky number which a DJ once told me was choreographed for beginning line dancers, to introduce them to a few of the basic steps. It also happens to be one of my cousin Jeff's favorite dances, so instead of leaving the dance floor, I crossed over to where he was and danced next to him. Though I'd moved away from my tall, blond admirer, I didn't mind, as once again I would have rather he watched me do a more challenging line dance— or perhaps a two-step.

I looked over my shoulder, past the other dancers to see my man working his way through the crowd at the edge of the floor. He was easy to spot, almost a head taller than the men around him. He moved all the way around the floor to the railing right in front of me, still staring and smiling.

After a few sequences—to prove to him I knew the dance well—I stepped over to him and told him he was not allowed to stare unless he got out and danced. He told me he didn't know how to dance but loved watching me. So I touched his beautiful, square chin, smiled, and continued dancing next to Jeff, feeling as if I had never before known the joy of movement.

After "Boxcar" I stood near a fan and cooled off. I smiled through the crowd a few times at the blond guy, and each smile seemed to work like a magic spell on him. After staring and staring, he finally approached. He introduced himself as Raymond, and it turned out that we had a mutual friend whom Raymond had been asking about me. Our friend had not known that I was recently single, and when I told this to Raymond, he was delighted.

During the next hour Raymond's seduction was overt, even including sexual descriptions he thought I wanted to hear. I thought his attentions were charming. I was attracted to him physically, and his aggressive come-ons made me feel desirable. A coworker, Adam, whispered to me that he found Raymond very attractive, and he kept trying to insert himself into our conversation. He even said, with an insincere-sounding laugh, that Raymond should leave me alone and pay attention to him instead.

Raymond ignored Adam, and he continued selling himself to me. I told him I was not looking for anything in particular and asked what he sought. His answer: a white picket fence, dogs, cats, horses, a garden, and pigs for slaughter.

Night 2

Things moved pretty fast. After the first night together, Raymond talked about wanting to tie me to his bed so I could never get away, about wanting me to be his boyfriend for the next ten or twenty years. I was getting a read off him that he was a bit rehearsed, a player with all the lines. I hesitated, not wanting to open up too quickly. I had learned years earlier not to put much stock into vows made in bed. But it wasn't in bed; it was in a parking lot where Raymond started to say, "I love you."

He got as far as, "I lo—"

It totally disarmed me. I had serious doubts about whether I could trust him. Still, when I heard the first two letters of that four-letter word, I felt nothing but desire.

One week after first spotting him at Hoedown's, we returned for our first night out as an official couple. Raymond looked totally handsome, with his 33-36 button-fly jeans, black boots, flannel shirt, and dark leather jacket. He looked even taller than the 6 foot 4 inches he claimed to be.

With my defenses crumbling under the relentlessness of this smart, funny, handsome, rugged man, I asked, as we climbed into his jeep to go to Hoedown's, "Should I run? Or should I run?" He said I should trust him, he was "safe to fall for." Then he fired up his jeep, gunned the engine, and screeched out of his lot, at the same time pulling two beers from the inside pocket of his jacket. I held on for what I knew would be an interesting ride.

As we walked into Hoedown's from the parking lot, I wondered whether Raymond would be affectionate, distant, attentive, or mean inside the club. Just as I was wondering, he told me he was unsure how to act with me, whether to ignore me or hang on me. I told him, "Do whatever feels natural." He grabbed my hand.

We were inseparable inside the club. Raymond was affectionate and attentive. I saw many handsome guys, but I was into my man, and he was into me. It was an awesome feeling to be led by the hand through the crowd by a great-looking guy. I loved the look of him from behind, with his short blond hair, his leather jacket, and his height.

Early in the evening Raymond pulled me aside and kissed my neck until I had a big, dark hickey. Friends told me they got bad vibes from Raymond, but I ignored them. Adam from work was there again, and he again shot Raymond coy looks. Eventually, Adam, frustrated, pinched my right tit, which I'd recently had pierced. The pain was instant, and I pulled away, yelping. Raymond stepped up quickly, towering over Adam with a threatening look. He told me later he had been ready to "kick Adam's ass for hurting my baby."

When they played "Boot Scoot Boogie," I danced at the edge of the dance floor. Raymond stood at the rail, and we stared at one another, just like we had done a week earlier.

Night 3

After knowing me 16 days, Raymond introduced the L word

in its entirety. I was not initially able to respond in kind, but he said I did not have to right away. I had discovered so much about him. Some things, like his refusal to take prescribed lithium for a manic-depressive diagnosis and his being on probation for assaulting an ex-boyfriend, should have been gigantic red flags. But there was an attraction that overwhelmed my anxiety. I was not desperate, but I craved him desperately.

He told me he loved me so many times that after one especially intense lovemaking session, I couldn't help but answer.

If only I had known what would happen on our third trip to Hoedown's, our second as a couple. Raymond and I met Jeff at the door. It was a dream come true. Raymond was handsome; we were the perfect couple in our cowboy hats and boots, him leading me aggressively through the bar by the hand. Other men were jealous. I had no desire to two-step with any of them, and I didn't mind that Raymond didn't know how to dance. I was content just to be with him.

A Texan I once knew told me that single men, when wearing button-fly jeans, should leave the bottom button undone to signify availability. Doing so had become an unconscious habit for me. But that night at Hoedown's, in the back corner, Raymond reached down and buttoned it. "You're no longer available," he told me.

At one point Raymond turned to the bartender to order our beers, and I leaned over to Jeff and whispered, "I am so in love." I was. It was so perfect, I decided to resign myself to the feeling.

The euphoria lasted about five minutes, until Raymond dropped a bomb on me. He said, in a very offhand way, something about having made out with Adam one of the few nights we were apart. He didn't sound remorseful but smug. I stepped back in disbelief and walked away, grabbing the first familiar man with whom I could two-step, blindly pulling him onto the dance floor.

My partner and I rounded the floor only once before Raymond grabbed my arm and pulled me off the dance floor, through the crowd, out the door, and into the parking lot. Raymond and I had a screaming match, but he refused to offer me any explanations or apologies. I stormed back into the club, and Raymond left. I was so hurt and mad I couldn't even think. My perfect evening had turned into the worst night ever.

A darkly handsome cowboy, Don, was obviously very interested in me, but I could hardly even think to flirt. Jeff tried comforting me, but without any explanation for events, I couldn't find words to speak. Bewildered, I left Jeff, Don, and Hoedown's and drove by Raymond's place. Not home. On my way back to Hoedown's, I saw his jeep in the parking lot of another club, the Heretic. I went in, wanting to talk, and found him making out like I didn't even exist.

I wheeled him around and hit him in the face. When he didn't strike back, I hit him again, unafraid of his size or his documented brawling experience. He spun around, so I kicked him in the ass. Then I hit him in the face again, calling him names. The crowd was staring, oddly silent. I left, pushing stunned onlookers out of my way. I sped back to Hoedown's and found Jeff, and we headed to my house. On the drive there Raymond called my cell phone and told me he had filed assault charges against me. He told me I was going to jail.

I wanted to know why he would do this to me, but he would not talk to me. He hung up on me, and I got no answers. I did not sleep that night. I just kept replaying things in my mind, against my will. My nerves were shot, and I waited for the police to arrive. (Raymond never actually filed charges.) In the morning Jeff and I went to get something to eat, but I couldn't swallow. I knew Raymond was getting off on the drama of our situation, playing the victim masterfully. All that day he called repeatedly to threaten me with arrest and to play the martyr. It jarred me when at the end of one conversation he said, "I love you."

Night 4

Thus started a pattern of strange, cyclical behavior. There would be intense romance for a few days, then he would insult me, stand me up, or threaten me. I would leave, and he would bombard me with sweet voice and e-mail messages.

As bizarre as his behavior was, my decision to stay with him was equally baffling. During one argument I told him my friends believed I was staying with him for purely physical reasons and that he would do nothing but continue to hurt me. Raymond's answer was that love is all about hurt.

That was when I decided to end things for good, and I warned Raymond against any further contact. I relied on the support of my friends in the days that followed. My body was in withdrawal, craving Raymond's long, lean body with tangible intensity. Jeff and I went out on the weekends, and everywhere we went, I prayed I would not see Raymond, unsure my body could resist his allure.

One warm night Jeff and I went to Hoedown's. We were sitting on a low wall in front of the club, drinking Cokes and resting after some dances. Hoedown's was crowded and hot, and the cool air felt refreshing. I said to Jeff, "I really hope we don't see you-know-who tonight."

At that moment, as if on cue, up walked Raymond. My insides froze when I saw how handsome he looked in his T-shirt, with a long-sleeved, unbuttoned, untucked shirt over that, cowboy hat, and boots—so different from my cutoff jeans shorts, T-shirt, and ball cap. Raymond looked eight feet tall and butch. He had let his goatee grow to a full beard, which I loved.

He stepped up to us, but Jeff and I stayed seated. I was unsure what to expect. Raymond leaned over and kissed me. Surprised, I did not respond, so he kissed me again and again until I kissed him back.

He apologized for the meanness and the fights. He told me he loved me and wanted me to call. He said he had wanted to call me but couldn't. He said he wanted me back.

Jeff and I glanced at one another with amazement.

Raymond continued to tell me he loved me; he had gotten his left tit pierced to complement mine. He pulled me up by the arm and lifted me to him so our nipple jewelry touched through our clothes. He told me I belonged with him and that I was the sweetest boy in the world—when I wasn't toying with his heart.

Raymond watched as I did line dances and two-steps with other men. At the end of one dance, a friend casually kissed me on the lips. Minutes later Raymond made sure I saw him kissing someone. So I decided to ignore him.

I was cooling off alone in the same corner of the bar where Raymond had once buttoned my jeans when he cornered me. He pushed me against the wall, forcing kisses on me. I pushed against him as he twisted my nipples and tried to mark my neck.

He kept telling me he loved me, and at one point, out of habit, I said, "I love you too." He asked why I broke up with him, and I told him I was afraid of him. His answer was that he'd never kill me. Maybe hurt me, but not kill me.

I gasped, told him I didn't want to be hurt either. I stumbled away, saying something about how it must feel terrible for him to not know love without pain. He grabbed my arm, pulled me back into the corner with him and started crying. A man nearby stepped up and asked if I was all right. I nodded, but then

Raymond pushed the guy away. He continued crying, grabbing me and holding me while muttering about our sex, his
loneliness, my looks. I wanted to comfort him, but when he
told me I had to prove to him that I loved him, a lightbulb
switched on in my head. This was a game for Raymond. I
somehow excused myself and got back to the dance floor.

During "Boot Scoot Boogie" Raymond strode onto the
dance floor as if I were the only dancer. He grabbed me suddenly, kissed me forcefully on the mouth, and said one final
time, "I'm your husband, and I love you." Then he turned
around and left Hoedown's. I made it through the rest of the
dance, not even hearing the music.

Night 5

It was not "Boot Scoot Boogie" but "Mambo Shuffle." I
saw him watching me, so I smiled. He smiled back, his eyes
fixed on me. I nodded, and he shook his head and grinned, as
if he couldn't believe he had caught my attention. He was
taller than Raymond—at least six and a half feet tall—and even
more muscular and masculine. At the end of the dance, he met
me at the bar and put his arm around my shoulders. "My
name's Wil," he told me. "I love watching you dance."

Once on Christmas Eve
by J. G. Hayes

Christmas Eve, and five of us were in a bar. Separately. Christmas can unify, they say, but not on this night. Not for us, anyway. We must have been the equal and opposite reaction to all the red-and-white happiness glittering elsewhere. The bartender watched the glare of a basketball game on the television perched at the bar's end. An overweight businessman sat three stools down from me, and his angle of slumping declination increased with each drink. On the end stool, swathed in shadow, sat that most forlorn of gay-bar denizens, a senior citizen. Everything about him seemed to have withered except his eyes, which caught mine in the mirror. Dust and ashes, ashes and dust, all is vanity. I saw in him my future—provided I survived the plague.

The mid-30-ish guy—my own age, I guessed—sat four stools away in the other direction. I had seen the bitterness of the evening falling from the folds of his tweed overcoat when he entered the bar some 20 minutes earlier. He was still wrapped loosely in the coat, and on his lap perched a large box done in red and gold Christmas foil with a now-crushed green bow on top. Like the rest of us, he kept his eyes frozen forward.

Dizzy strings of red bulbs crisscrossed the smoky ceiling. Multicolored lights chased each other around the edges of the bar's plate-glass mirror. Holiday music set to a frenzied disco beat waltzed across the empty dance floor behind us—mourning those who weren't there, mocking those who were. As the songs and their upbeat lyrics played, my mood shifted from amused irony to desperation.

The businessman shook to life and ordered another drink. The bartender grudgingly obliged; one sensed he had somewhere else to go this evening, unlike, apparently, the rest of us. I turned my eyes downward in the face of his scorn but raised my forefinger nonetheless. Another shot of oblivion, please. And yet I never could quite get there.

Perhaps the holidays' nastiest trick is its command to recall, to relive, to remember. And with alcohol eagerly greasing the skids, my mind slid back 30 years, stopping at a long-ago Christmas the way a jukebox set at random culls a selection totally unexpected but totally familiar.

I was 5 and stepping out our old back door into a world made dazzling and supreme by a foot of snow the evening before. Christmas Day. Neither impassable roads nor a passel of oversugared children stopped my parents from bundling us out to Aunt Anne's in the country. Everyone was with me, spilling out the door. I could hear their voices. Mom's clear laugh. Dad still young and handsome and alive, picking out targets for brother Bob to hit with snowballs. The girls gushing over the clothes and dolls they'd just received. And me, the youngest, shocked into muteness by the triple sublimity of a snowstorm, Christmas Day, and an upcoming ride on the mysterious subway. My kaleidoscope of delight spun beautifully as the day unfurled like a flower, from the new snow-white coats of the too-tall pines to the racehorse game my mother magically produced once we were tucked into our rumbling subway seats. And then Aunt Anne's. A gaggle of relations hugging me. Wizened old relatives mesmerizing me with tales of wonder and woe. Strange new cousins to play with. The smell of 40 different delights melding into one in Aunt Anne's kitchen—slow-basted turkey, gingerbread, orange peel on the fire, mulled cider. And Aunt Anne's secret stairway leading to the attic, where still-wrapped presents for her nephews and nieces glittered like just-discovered continents, limitless in their potential.

Back at the bar I watched my cigarette smoke spiral upward and wondered where those halcyon days went—for there was weight to them. Surely they were more than nothing. I looked at the candy-colored liquor bottles lined up like toy soldiers and wondered, *Are they really there?* And then my eyes refocused, and I saw the young man in the overcoat, his profile—handsome—reflected in the mirror, staring at nothing. His gaily-wrapped package by this time had fallen on the floor, and I got the feeling it was doomed to stay there, like treasure at the bottom of a cold, cold sea. And he was crying. Softly, almost silently. Yet somehow this pitiful sound filtered through the dueling cacophony of television and music. Perfectly audible.

But, say what you will, the holidays give us license to do…if not great things, then good things. So, because it was Christmas and I could get away with it, I abandoned my bar stool and approached the crying man. I sat on the stool next to him.

We stared forward at our own solemn reflections. He continued his quiet crying. But we reached for each other, and our hands met and clasped halfway between the immeasurable distance that separated us.

Silently we sat, hand in hand, staring straight ahead, the din

of the disco and the drone of the television falling hard all
around us. And still he cried.

At last he turned to me, and I turned to him. We stared at
each other for a moment. Then he reached to the ground, re-
trieved his package, and handed it to me.

"Merry Christmas," he said.

In Search of Local Wildlife at the Gizmo Lounge
by Ron Suresha

One dusty, sweaty afternoon in the summer of '82, I was heading west across Alabama, leaving one lousy job in hopes of finding another somewhere better. I was driving my old red Valiant—with the slant six you just couldn't kill, no matter how hard you ran it—heading from Atlanta to Houston. The back seat was loaded with everything I owned: a beat-up suitcase, a box each of books and papers, and a cooler full of soda and beer. Actually, I could have stashed everything into the trunk and used the room in the back seat to accommodate randy hitchhikers. But I hadn't thought of that when I packed.

I decided to stop for the night in the fine Southern city of Birmingham. Didn't know anyone in Birmingham—or in all of the grand state of Alabama, for that matter—but I couldn't afford a hotel, and the rest stops I'd seen didn't look as if they'd be safe to park or hang out at all night long.

I'd driven about eight hours that day and was bushed, but I had a plan. I figured I'd just get out my U.S. gay bar guide, glide into the nearest men's bar for a tall cold one, and check out the local wildlife. If there was a decent-looking guy, I'd flirt a bit and wait for an overnight invitation.

I stopped just before dusk at the last rest stop before the city. Inside the dank john, some short stocky trucker (his rig heading the other way, I'd noticed outside) came up to the piss hole next to mine and watched me shake off the dew from my lily. He wasn't half bad-looking, from what I could see out of the corner of my eye. Daylight was fading, however, and my first thought was to save myself for tonight's host, whoever that might be.

As I flushed and zipped up, he turned and looked, and I gave him the nod meaning, *Sure, I'm interested, but I can't right now,* and went back to my car. I sat in the back seat, lit a smoke, and fished out my bar guide from the box.

There were only a couple of gay bars listed in Birmingham, out of a total of four or so bars in the whole state. Reading the entries was hardly encouraging, but at least it wasn't nothing. The Gizmo Lounge sounded OK, so I wrote the address on a scrap of paper and tossed the book back in its box. That's when it struck me that I hadn't a city map or any idea how the hell to get to the Gizmo.

As I got out of the back seat, I noticed the trucker that had cruised me in the john was eyeing me again from up in his cab. By the way his shoulders were moving, I could tell he was priming the pump. I looked above the truck at the low-hanging clouds on this sultry late afternoon, locked my car, and headed to the truck for directions.

Twenty minutes later I stepped out of the truck with a hand-drawn map. The trucker blew his air horn and geared up and out. I followed him halfway out of the rest stop, flashed my lights, and took the west-bound split.

With the trucker's map it wasn't hard at all to find the Gizmo. Birmingham wasn't all that big a city, at least compared to cities I'd lived in up north. I got in right as the darkness was settling. There were only few cars in the parking lot, and mine was the lone out-of-state plate.

Being from out of town in a bar has its pluses and minuses. On the plus side, all the townies think of you as fresh meat; on the minus side, if it's not a friendly place, you can be downright unwelcome. Either way, I was up for the challenge, and I was sure ready for a break from the long road.

In the car I combed my hair, checked my beard, adjusted my basket. I made a flash assessment of the bar as I walked up: a stand-alone building, longer than wide, no windows in front or on either side, and, in back, a fenced-in patio.

I pulled the door and stepped in. Patsy Cline's crooning floated into my ears as I stood and blinked around for a minute. The place was surprisingly spacious, with separate areas for the pool tables (two guys standing around one of them), booths (vacant), dance floor (also vacant), and squarish center bar (five customers and a bartender).

I headed for a seat with a view of the entire place and noticed that several of the men were watching me. It felt as if the place was frozen in stop-action. I smiled and nodded to nobody in particular as I approached the bar and heard the bartender say, "Howdy, there. What'll you have?" *Good service,* I thought, dropping my butt onto the bar stool.

"Gotta draft?" I asked, and the bartender came into focus, smiling. He was an older man, maybe 50, with a big droopy mustache and a slight stoop in his wide shoulders.

"You betcha," he said and winked. As he turned to fetch a glass, a guy on the other side of the bar, looking maybe 50, with silver hair, held up a bill and called out, "I got this one, Don. Don't often get such good-lookin' men here in town. Isn't that right, Don?" "Hardly never," said the bartender. Then the other guy smiled broadly and addressed me: "Where ya from, stranger?"

So much for blending in unnoticed, I thought. I gave my name—though he'd asked where I was from—and thanked him for the beer, to which he said, "Pleased t'meetcha, Ron. I'm Harold."

The bartender set my beer down in front of me and offered a thick hand. "Hiya, Ron, welcome to the Giz. I'm Don, the owner. Don't let ol' Harold get to you."

"I ain't botherin' him none, ya ol' goat! Just bought 'im a beer, fer chrissakes." I felt a vague sense of being stared at but ignored it. Harold said, "Izzit 'gainst some kinda law fer bein' friendly?" Don just smiled and shook his head. Then Harold, the silver-haired welcome wagon, proceeded to introduce everyone else in the bar.

Three seats to Harold's right perched Al, curly haired, neatly dressed, with a bubba belly. He looked like an insurance agent with a passion for crème-filled doughnuts. He nodded and gave a fey little wave.

Directly across from me sat a tall, lanky fellow in overalls named Zeke (*you've got to be kidding,* I thought; *what a name*) who nodded across the bar at me with bright eyes but then shyly dropped his gaze back to his beer mug. He wasn't bad-looking but shifted his elbows awkwardly, as if his arms didn't quite fit his torso, and so came off gawky and self-conscious.

Further around the bar, about four seats to my left, was Andy, the most down-and-out–looking of the group, maybe 22 or so, slightly bloated and blotchy-skinned. When I turned to look at him, he stared blankly at me, with a lit match held to his smoke and about to burn his fingers.

"And them two shooting pool," continued Harold, pointing behind Andy, "are Kenny and Truman." They were dressed almost identically, in worn jeans and white T-shirts. When Harold introduced them, Kenny, trim and about 25, smiled at me and then turned and giggled at Truman, who looked like a well-fed former farm boy about ten years Kenny's senior. Truman grunted at Kenny and said to me, "Don't pay *her* no mind, y'hear? Just actin' silly. Silly as a goose." Then turning back to his pool shot, Truman snipped at Kenny, "Jes' lookit yew, yew silly goose."

And finally, a few seats to my right sat Jake, the best-looking of the bunch. Jake was about as beefy as most of the others but more muscular, with a squarish jaw and small mustache. He wore a blue T-shirt tight enough to outline his nipples. "A real pleasure t'meetcha," he said in a deep resonant drawl. Jake was the only one to get out of his seat to greet me. His handshake was firm and warm and slightly moist, and his eyes revealed more than casual interest.

"All righty, now," resumed Harold. "Now that you met the whole gang here, whyn't you tell us 'bout yerself? Where ya from?"

Al piped in, "Where y'headin'? Whatcha doin' here in our fair city?"

"Oh come on, guys," interrupted Don, "he's jes' barely set his butt up on the chair 'afore you go an' give him the third degree. Give the man a break, why dontcha?"

The guys retorted back, but I quickly interrupted in a friendly tone, "Now, Don, let 'em be. I don't mind, really I don't." Not wanting to betray myself as a Yank and with the benefit of the slight drawl I'd acquired during my years in Georgia, I simply said I was from Atlanta. And I went on to explain—to the whole group, I realized mid sentence, as everyone seemed to be craning their ears my way—my bad luck at jobs, my road trip, and finding the place from the guidebook. The guys alternately nodded, smiled, clucked sympathetically, and chuckled, adding comments back and forth across the bar.

It struck me that not only were they unusually friendly to strangers but that they talked among themselves (and with me) as if they were all in the same group, even though spread throughout the bar. None of them, except maybe Kenny and Truman, were holding private conversations. Even Zeke, the quietest, and Andy, the drunkest, would pipe in from time to time.

As I figured, most of the men were blue-collar and nearly half were out of work, for one reason or another. "Most near ever'body who lives here is from here," said Harold. It seemed that Don, who'd owned the bar for about four years, was the only man there completely out of the closet at work and to his family. The rest proclaimed themselves "Southern bachelors" to their coworkers and family.

Even though Harold was the biggest flirt there, it turned out he lived with his partner of almost 20 years, who had been his best friend in high school. The two of them had double-dated a laundry list of local girls, never managing to find the ones they wanted to settle down with—as their frustrated fondness for each other grew and grew. Finally, after more than ten years, Harold and his buddy got drunk and stoned enough to go skinny-dipping one night at a nearby stone quarry. When they climbed out of the water, their mutual arousal was so apparent that neither could ignore it. Despite the risk of being discovered, they had sex right there and then. Two days later they moved in together.

Jake was an out-of-work mechanic trying to make ends meet by working nights at 7-Eleven. In his sexy drawl he explained, "I moved to the big city because, as sad as gay life in Birmingham may be, there ain't a lick of it in Tuscaloosa." Then he talked a little about his elderly mother and the house he'd rented for them to live in. "Other'n that, there's not much to tell here." My hopes dipped a tad when Jake said he lived with his ma, since I thought he'd be my best prospect for shacking up that night. *But,* I thought to myself, *don't worry, just bide your time.*

Andy, also not working, lived with his sister and brother-in-law. He hadn't much to say, but his tipsy voice and red-ringed eyes spoke of an early hell. I avoided having to hear his sorry story by excusing myself to hit the head.

There was a full mug of cold beer waiting for me when I returned. "On the house," said Don.

"I could sure get used to having a bar like this around," I replied, and held the brew in toast to everyone. "Damn right friendly folks here."

With a little squirm Al continued the circle of storytelling. "Well, I sell used cars, is all. Lived here all m'life. Lookin' fer a boyfriend, y'know. Like most ever'body else round here, I think." He slugged down the last of his beer and held it out to Don, saying, "I just wanna Bud, is all." Don replaced his beer. "But most guys don't stay here who can run off elsewheres, New Orleans or 'Lanta. Been to 'Lanta myself, 'bout five years back. Couldn't-a ever lived there, is all. Sure were plenty o' good-lookin' boys, though." He crossed his eyes and struck a demented pose. "But them folk jest plumb crazy up thar!" Which brought a round of agreeable laughter.

Kenny and Truman had lived together for four years in Birmingham, having landed there after living in some little bum-fuck town near Mobile. Following an extended secret sexual affair—Truman was Kenny's boss at a local grocery and married with three kids—was a frightening episode when Kenny's father, a farmer of some sort, found the pair naked in the family barn and nearly shot them both. They'd hightailed it out of town that very night, with barely a suitcase between them. It sounded harrowing, but to hear them tell it, you'd

think it was a matter of course. "The wages you pay for love,"
giggled Kenny. Nowadays Truman worked as a short-order
cook. Kenny, I suspected, was the gracious housewife.

Just as I was about to ask Zeke to tell *his* story, Harold got
up and whispered to Al. Al nodded and stood. Then Harold
asked if I'd seen the patio in back of the bar—a question that
set the whole bar in motion. Zeke and Andy headed to the
back of the bar. Truman and Kenny followed. "Why, no," I
said, a mite reluctantly, "can't say I have."

Harold approached me and said in a low tone of voice, "A
few of us're goin' back to have a lil' smoke, if y'know what I
mean, an' yer more'n welcome to join us."

"Oh, well, thanks 'n' all that, but I don't know...."

"It's a *fabulous* ol' space out there. The best lil' patio in the
South!"

I hedged, not wanting to seem ungrateful or ungracious but
unsure about being around drugs in that locale. Almost everyone else was already out the back door.

Don intervened. "Oh, jes' leave him be, Harold. If he wants
to join you, he will, that's all."

Harold, looking a bit crushed, started back to the patio.
Over his shoulder he winked, "Well, if y'change yer mind,
you know where t'find us."

I was left alone with Don, wiping glasses clean with a white
bar rag and Dan Seals on the jukebox. Don turned to me and
started talking about the bar. He told me a little bit about its
history and about the small gay community in Bram, as the locals call it. Because the Giz was one of the few gay bars—and
probably the largest—in the state, gays would drive there from
an hour or even further away.

As he was talking about the bar, without looking up from
his cleaning, Don remarked casually, "Y'know, it's perfectly

safe out there, if you wanted to check it out."

"Well, I could stand to stretch my legs a spell." After my second beer, I could hear my Atlanta-acquired drawl thickening. "Maybe I'll wander on out back there for a minute or two."

Don smiled and went back to polishing glasses.

When I got out to the patio, I was surprised to see that it was quite a nice little setup. Small trees and potted plants ringed the area. There were plenty of benches and tables. The lighting was neither bright nor dim. And music from the jukebox was piped out to the patio at a reasonable volume. I was impressed that such a hole could be so pleasant.

"Jes' in time," Howard said to me as he lit up a joint. The pungent smoke cut the night air like scissors slicing velvet. The whole group breathed it in at once and exhaled in unison. The air was warm and the canopy of stars glimmered like a canvas filled with rhinestones.

Andy said, "Now, don't that smell purty?"

We nodded or hummed our agreement, and the joint made its way around the circle. The first time I passed, but the second time around I took a hit. The men's voices got soft and low. I admired aloud the patio and appreciated the company.

One joint was finished and another was lit. The conversation became general, talking about the weather and some such, and I was about to strike up a one-on-one conversation with Jake when Howard's semishrill voice disrupted the relative quiet.

"Well, now, hey, there, Ron. I guess you've never seen our good friend's Zeke's dong, have you?"

I don't get fazed easily, but that comment sure caught me off guard. I looked at Zeke, standing a bit off to my left. He was blushing. "Uh, no," I said, "can't say I have."

"Oh, yeah, you gotta see the pud on Zeke! It's really something! Hoo-wee!" said Howard. And before I knew it, all the rest of the group was exclaiming and laughing and encouraging Zeke.

For his part, Zeke just shuffled his feet and bashfully looked down at them, his hands stuck deep into his overalls pockets like a little kid who'd been asked to tap dance for his relatives. "Aw, heck, he don't wanna see that ol' thang none," he stammered.

The men persisted, "Course he does! You oughta catch Zeke's big ol' wanger, Ron! C'mon Zeke, jes' give us a lil' peek, hmm?" They acted as if Zeke were some sort of tourist attraction, and even though my curiosity was stoked, I wasn't sure I wanted them taunting the guy on my account.

"Look, it's fine," I said. "If he doesn't wanna do it, let him be." This seemed to quiet them down a bit. When I looked back at Zeke, though, with his head down and feet shuffling, he was smiling.

"Well," Zeke said at last with a sly grin, "awright. But jes' fer a minute." He didn't need much encouragement, after all.

Zeke unbuttoned the sides of his pants. He undid one of the buttons on the front flap of his overalls, and then the other. The flap fell forward, exposing his T-shirt and a lean, tight belly. Holding the straps, he slowly lowered his pants. Apparently Zeke didn't bother with undershorts.

The guys were poised, staring as Zeke exposed his bush. A few of the guys muttered "Yeah" or "All righty, now," but otherwise we held our breath. Zeke dropped his pants to the top of the root of his organ. We were, to a man, spellbound— like johns at a strip joint. Then, pretending to have to switch his hold on the straps, he hiked his overalls a few inches higher, causing his audience to groan in frustration. It was obvious that Zeke had done this before and that he was working it for all its worth.

"Awright, awright, already," grinned Zeke. "Hold onna yer

cocks, I'm gettin' there." So he continued to lower his pants, past his bush to the top of the base and then, pausing again briefly for effect, lower and lower, showing inch after fat inch of soft male pipe. At the four-inch mark, with no head in sight, Kenny giggled and said, "My, my, my." Zeke paused a second, then kept going. Another three inches or so. I let out a long low whistle. Then, after another three inches, Zeke's huge glans finally emerged. Then, in one movement, he let his over-alls drop to the floor.

Harold shrieked. Kenny turned his eyes away, pretending to swoon. The others hooted and gasped appreciatively. I stood there with my jaw down to my chest, shaking my head. "Holy shit," I said. "Ain't that the biggest fuckin' snake you ever laid yer eyes on?"

Zeke reached over to where he'd set his beer, picked it up, and drained it. Then he pulled his overalls up. "Show's over, guys. Sorry." He started back into the bar and everyone followed.

Taking my seat, I thanked Zeke for his lack of modesty and offered to buy him a beer. Surprisingly, he once again turned shy and unassuming, saying, "Shucks, sure, thanks a bunch."

The gang was settling back into their places, greeting a few other locals who'd turned up while we were on the patio. "You got a boyfriend who takes care of that monster for you?" I asked Zeke.

"Naw," he replied. "Ain't nobody'll go near it, let alone try t'do anythin' with the freakin' thang. It's just awful sometimes 'cause everybody in these parts knows. Town this small, word gets round."

I was about to offer some words of sympathy, but Jake interrupted in his increasingly sexy drawl to introduce me to the new arrivals. Then, in a while, more folks came in—including some of the local wimmin—and the conversations broke up into smaller groups around the bar. Jake made a point of introducing me around, and I suspect I met just about every gay man and lesbian from Bram that memorable night.

I wish I could say I took on Zeke. But I didn't. I never got the chance. About an hour after the patio incident, just as Jake was telling me in that deep sexy voice of his that his ma was visiting his sister in Tuscaloosa, I glimpsed Zeke. With his head down he quietly slipped out the front door of the Gizmo Lounge and into the cooling Alabama night.

One for the Road
by M. Christian

"Roger," I say, raising my half-full shot, amber rolling back and forth, miniature breakers on shores of ice.

Laughing. I remember most of all his laugh, a rumble that carried across the most crowded of rooms. Roger hadn't laughed a lot. He'd been stone butch and laughed only when something slithered through his pumped armor and tickled him. But when he did laugh it was a sound that stopped everything. Everyone looked for the roaring, barking lion.

"Joe," says the bartender, turning his bottles, looking for imminent empties.

Quiet. It's been easy to not miss Joe. Soft and silent, his passion ran deep. Some made fun of him or worse, ignored him. Because of his shyness, his silence. But he had a family that was with him through all of his and all of their shit. They were able to talk to Joe and not the frightened boy, terrified of speaking in public. His family went up his stairs and through his door and saw the paintings—the real Joe, full of color, brilliance, anger, humor, sex, perception, and voice. The ultimate privilege for those that knew him is to have him—the real him—hanging in their homes.

"Peter," I say, taking a sip, feeling the crisp burn slide to my already warm stomach.

Sharp. Peter had been a character. Best way of saying it, the perfect way, always chiming in with something witty, catty—always with the razor comment. Peter had taken the mantel of bitchy queen and pushed it past cliché to *King Lear*'s Fool. He left a wave of lies, illusions, and polite hypocrisy in his wake.

"Mandy" says the bartender, cleansing the spouts with a burst of hot water and a paper towel.

Trixie. Mandy was really Trixie. Trixie was really Mandy. Friends used to worry about him, about how the little office manager Mandy was so one way—Shakespeare in the Park, free days at the DeYoung, season tickets for the opera, first edition prints—and Trixie was the other—loud, rude, brash, feathers, squealing, dancing with straight sailors on Halloween. The gap he leaves could only be filled by two.

"Josh" I say, looking again at the gold in my glass, watching the overheads play in the cubes.

Young. But I remember him old. Josh was old. You could see it in his eyes. He'd gather his special friends together, join hands, raise energy, call the corners, thank the goddess. He'd pass the wine and the bread, baby-fine hands and ash-blond hair. A baby playing dress up. But when he spoke the words and chimed the bell and lit the candle, Tibetan plains reflected in his clear blue eyes; African plains howled in his voice; he gestured like the Buddha. Everyone knows he'll be back, but that doesn't mean we don't miss him now.

"Tommy," says the bartender, cutting a lemon neatly.

Wrong. No one called him Tommy. True, his license said Tommy and his mother said Tommy—tears shining her face—but that was wrong. If you knew him, you knew him black and leather, sneer and command, toys and the sound of fleshy impacts. It might have been Tommy, formally, as people cried, but everyone really misses Sir.

"Matt," I say, downing my glass, strong and tart, tickling my tongue. Tumbling.

"Matt?" says the bartender, putting his knife down. "I didn't know about Matt. Didn't even know he was positive."

I shake my head, sad. "Liver went. Tried to dry out but not in time."

The bartender nods. "Another?"

Contributor Biographies

Mark C. Abbott, a native of a Buffalo, N.Y., and then Central Florida B.D. (Before Disney) has lived in or around Washington, D.C., for almost 30 years. He worked as a federal bureaucrat and now works as a copy editor.

Kevin Bentley is a writer and editor living in San Francisco. His creative nonfiction has appeared in *ZYZZYVA, Diseased Pariah News, His 2, Flesh & the Word 4,* and *Obsessed.*

Ethan Brandon is the pen name of a college communications and theater professor and former broadcaster. A native of Rochester, N.Y., he currently teaches at a small college in West Tennessee, where he lives with his two cats and near his incredibly supportive circle of friends.

Joe Frank Buckner is a short-story writer currently working on a novel. He lives on a Florida island.

Blaise Bulot divides his time between Boston and New Orleans. He has had two writing careers: The first produced over 100 scholarly and scientific publications, including three advanced chemistry textbooks, one so good the Soviets pirated it.

In more recent years he has had short stories, poetry, and articles on gay, racial, and civil rights issues published. He has self-published two gay novels, *Dark Waters* and *Starr Lyte,* and he reviews nonfiction for *The Lambda Book Report.*

M. Christian's work can be found in *Best American Erotica, Best Gay Erotica,* and *The Mammoth Book of Historical Erotica* as well as many other books and magazines. He is the editor of *Eros Ex Machina, Midsummer Night's Dreams, Guilty Pleasures,* and coeditor, with Simon Sheppard, of the forthcoming Alyson Publications anthology *Rough Stuff: Tales of Gay Men, Sex, and Power.*

Randy Clark lives in San Francisco. His story *Walking Past the Playing Fields* appeared last year in the Alyson anthology *Telling Tales Out of School.* In the 1980s he contributed to the gay radio show *Closet Free Radio* in Santa Cruz. He is an active member of the Gay and Lesbian Historical Society of Northern California, for which he created the Web site www.glhs.org.

Brian Cochran has not been to a gay bar in more than five years. He has written articles about culture, politics, and news for *Frontiers, Southern Voice, Opera News, The Front Page,* and *Dallas Voice.* His interview with cartoonist Lynn Johnston won an Honorable Mention at the 1997–98 Vice Versa Awards. He lives with his life partner near Atlanta.

Bob Condron has written and directed extensively for community and fringe theater with notable success. His short-format erotic fiction has been published in a variety of American and Canadian magazines and anthologies. His first full-length erotic novel, *Easy Money,* will be published in mid 1999. He lives and works in Berlin with his husbear of four years, Tom.

M. DeForge has routinely regaled his family and friends with his escapades in and around Washington, D.C., where he lived from 1970 to 1988. This is his first attempt at putting them down on paper. His desire to hang out in bars was extinguished in 1981, when he met his lover, Gary Wayne Mertine. After Gary's death in 1991, Duc moved from their home in Norfolk, Va., back to D.C., where he successfully trotted the boards in local community theater. M. DeForge currently resides in Moscow, Russia.

Dean Durber, English-born, has lived and traveled extensively throughout Asia, including a three-year stint as a teacher in rural Japan. For the past three years, he has offered fiction, travel, children's, and performance-art articles to a variety of publications around the world. He recently completed his first novel. A production of his new stage play *Rising From the Ashes: The story of River Phoenix* opened in Sydney, where he now resides, in February 1999.

Jack Fritscher, winner of the BEA National Small Press Book Award 1998–1999 for *Rainbow County and 11 Other Stories,* is the founding San Francisco editor of *Drummer,* the third gay magazine created after Stonewall. With more than 5,000 pages in print, this diversely voiced author of 12 books, with stories and feature articles in more than 25 gay magazines, is noted for the '90s novel about the 70s Golden Age of Liberation, *Some Dance to Remember,* as well as for his biographical memoir of his bicoastal lover, photographer Robert Mapplethorpe, entitled *Mapplethorpe: Assault With a Deadly Camera.* His Lammy-nominated novel, *The Geography of Women,* is an inclusive lesbigay story of extended family. His photographs, appearing in dozens of community magazines, often as covers and centerfolds, were introduced by British critic Edward Lucie-Smith in the coffee-table photo book *Jack Fritscher's American Men.*

J. G. Hayes is an ex-newspaperman living in the Boston area. He is currently working on a collection of short stories set in his native South Boston as well as a novel. He is the owner of Vision Landscape, a design-build firm serving clients in the Boston area.

Gene-Michael Higney is a transplanted New Yorker working as a television and film consultant and script doctor. He is author of numerous horror stories, one of which appears in the anthology *The Best of Cemetery Dance.*

Wayne Hoffman is a journalist whose reporting has appeared in dozens of publications, including *The Advocate, XY,* the *Boston Phoenix,* and *Torso.* He coedited the anthology *Policing Public Sex,* and his essays have appeared in *Generation Q, Men Seeking Men,* and *Boy Meets Boy.* He is currently the arts editor at the *New York Blade.* He is always taking notes, so watch what you say around him.

When he's not out "researching" the bar scene, Christopher Horan is a freelance writer and former political speechwriter living in Boston, where he works in public education. His short stories, essays, and poems have appeared in several literary journals.

Owen Levy is the author of the best-selling 1980s novel *A Brother's Touch.* A survivor of the Stonewall riots, until recently he lived in Berlin. He has been awarded resident fellowships by the Wurlitzer Foundation in Taos, N.M., and the Edwin MacDowell Colony in Peterborough, N.H. As a freelancer, his reviews, entertainment stories, and profiles have appeared in various gay and mainstream publications. He can be contacted via E-mail at 110213.1664@compuserve.com.

Chip Livingston is the author of the novel *Naming Ceremony*. He lives in Boulder, Colo. His writing has appeared in *The Advocate*, *The James White Review*, *Positively Native*, *The Raven Chronicles*, *The Harrisburg Review*, and other journals. He is currently working on a book of nonfiction.

Christopher Lucas has short stories published in *The Church Wellesley Review* and Gayplace.com. He bartends and is currently working on a novel. He currently lives in Albuquerque with his lover of more than seven years and their two dogs.

Mark Macdonald is a 28-year-old writer and artist living in Vancouver. He lives with his partner and cat in a bizarre love triangle and by day sells books at Little Sister's Book & Art Emporium.

David May was a nice boy from a good family who fell in with the wrong crowd. He is the author of the S/M-oriented *Madrugada*. His work, both fiction and nonfiction, has appeared in *The Harvard Gay & Lesbian Review*, *Advocate Men*, *Cat Fancy*, *Drummer*, *Frontiers*, *Honcho*, *Inches*, *International Leatherman*, *Lambda Book Report*, and *Mach*. His fiction also appears in the anthologies *Midsummer Night's Dreams*, *Cherished Blood*, *Flesh and the Word 3*, *Meltdown!*, *Queer View Mirror*, and *Rogues of San Francisco*. He lives in San Francisco with his husband, a dog, and two cats.

Ian-Andrew McKenzie lives and works near Atlanta. Previously published in the anthology *Queer View Mirror*, he has been working on his first novel for as long as he can remember.

Ernest McLeod has published stories in *The James White Review*, *The GSU Review*, *bananafish*, and *Men on Men 7*. When not coerced by his partner, Kevin Moss, to live in such far-flung places as Hungary and Russia, he writes and resides in Vermont. He has recently completed a collection of stories and is beginning work on a novel and a trio of travel novellas.

Jim Piazza is a lyricist, playwright, and regular contributor to *Out*. His one-man performance piece *Recline and Fall: Memoirs of an Uneasy Lay* is based on his forthcoming sexual autobiography.

Gregg Shapiro is a poet and fiction writer whose work has appeared in literary journals such as *Gargoyle, Faultline, Christopher Street, Modern Words, Evergreen Chronicles,* and *Spoon River Poetry Review* and the anthologies *Getting It On, Beyond Lament, Reclaiming the Heartland, Mondo Marilyn,* and *Mondo Barbie* as well as textbooks, including *Literature and Gender*. He lives in Chicago.

Ron Suresha is a writer and editor living in Boston. His writing has appeared or is scheduled to appear in *The Harvard Gay and Lesbian Review, In Newsweekly, American Bear, Gay Community News, Darshan,* and *Visionary* as well as the anthologies *My First Time 2, The Bear Book, Bear Book 2,* and *Straighter Than Straight*. He has also self-published a chapbook of recipes, *Mugs o' Joy*.

Michael A. White was born and raised in Ohio. For the past ten years he has lived in West Palm Beach, Fla., where he is a librarian in the county library system. He is 37 and still seeking a tan and a relationship that will last.